THE
HANGED MAN

Also by David Skibbins

THE STAR
HIGH PRIESTESS
EIGHT OF SWORDS

THE HANGED MAN

DAVID SKIBBINS

THOMAS DUNNE BOOKS
ST. MARTIN'S MINOTAUR
NEW YORK

THOMAS DUNNE BOOKS.
An imprint of St. Martin's Press.

THE HANGED MAN. Copyright © 2008 by David Skibbins. All rights reserved. Printed in the United States of America. For information, address St. Martin's Press, 175 Fifth Avenue, New York, N.Y. 10010.

On pages 217–18, "Strange" lyrics by Pollyanna Bush, © 2005. All rights reserved by Pollyanna Bush Music Company. Used with permission.

www.thomasdunnebooks.com
www.minotaurbooks.com

Library of Congress Cataloging-in-Publication Data

Skibbins, David, 1947–
    The hanged man : a tarot card mystery series novel / David Skibbins.—1st ed.
        p. cm.
    ISBN-13: 978-0-312-37783-0
    ISBN-10: 0-312-37783-5
    1. Ritter, Warren (Fictitious character)—Fiction.   2. Tarot—Fiction.   3. California—Fiction.   I. Title.

PS3619.K55 H36   2008
813'.6—dc22

                                                    2008018096

First Edition: August 2008

10 9 8 7 6 5 4 3 2 1

This book is dedicated to the founder, Markos Moulitsas Zúniga, and the wonderful community for progressive Democratic researchers, online journalists, and commentators who have created the Daily Kos (www.dailykos.com). Week after week, they scoop traditional media sources. They give us news from around the world, the stories that corporate-controlled mainstream media censors or spins. The Daily Kos truly represents the independent freethinking that embodies the American ideal. Warren and I salute them.

Acknowledgments

I couldn't write without the ongoing support of my parents, my daughter, my wife, my Portuguese water dog, and the warm community of fans and friends who inspire me to keep writing. Joel and Jeremy Crockett at Four-Eyed Frog Books not only hand sell my books, but help me edit my material. Special thanks to Pollyanna Bush for granting me permission to use the lyrics from her haunting ballad "Strange." The friendly folks who live in the small towns along this isolated stretch of Route 1 on the northern California coast bolster me up every day with their encouragement and caring. I am blessed.

0

THE NUMBER ZERO

IN NUMEROLOGY, Zero represents that which preceded all creation and that which shall exist after our universe disappears. It is boundless, nameless, limitless. It is the frame on which the wheel of karma spins. It is the ground from which everything arises, even death. Especially death.

PROLOGUE

Asphyxiation was delicious. The blindfold was snug, but not too tight. She'd used the small ball in his mouth so he could swallow OK. The soft cuffs didn't cut into his wrists or ankles. The earmuffs were a new thing, but they really left him alone and cut off. The collar was a little large, and chafed under his chin. But it meant that his neck would be safe when she cut off his air in their breath play. What an unexpected delight! He was hot just imagining what was coming.

He thought he heard a voice. He couldn't tell if it was her or someone else. A man? What was going on? This was supposed to be a private scene, just the two of them. Then he felt someone grab the lacings of his collar. Something was very wrong. He rapped his knuckles three times against the post: his red light signal. Why hadn't she taken off his blindfold? She had to stop right now. He rapped again.

Then he felt the jerk of the lacings. The collar was tightening, doing just what it was designed to do, cutting off his oxygen. But this was no play. He struggled against his cuffs. He tried to scream, but all that made it past the latex ball gag was a moan. He twisted his head back and forth, struggling for one precious breath. Explosive flashes burst inside his eyeballs. His chest strained against the ropes. A searing fire ripped through him as his heart tried for one last beat. Then nothing.

1

THE NUMBER ONE

ONE, IN occult traditions, stands for the prime mover, the initial thrust into being. It begins all action, all consciousness. Every story only exists in potential until that moment when One comes into being. Hence the phrase "Once upon a time . . ."

CHAPTER ONE

Did that hurt?"

Warren clawed his way free from the tentacles of his dream. A vampire was slashing his throat and sucking his blood. Awake, the bite on his neck still throbbed.

"You looked so adorable, lying there. I just had to give you a little nip. I think my teeth are sharper than I thought."

Sally's voice. He sighed. He was not about to join the eternal undead. He cranked open one eye. There in front of him was the freshest smile on the planet.

He said, "It's daytime. Doesn't sunlight kill your kind?"

She chuckled. "Good morning, Master Ritter. How did you sleep?"

"Sleep? Did we sleep?" He had both eyes open now. Sally was lying next to him, propped up on one arm, deliciously naked.

She said, "Yes, we did sleep, among other things. And on that topic, do you have any more things to show me?" She was ready for a rematch. Time for a lesson in harsh reality.

"Sally, nothing works for me very well hydraulically until my first hit of caffeine. Or cognitively, or emotionally, or just about any other word ending in *ly* that you can think of."

She said, "Don't move, I'll be right back." Then she sat up, hoisted herself into her chair, and wheeled out of the bedroom.

He lay there wondering if that morning's dental salutation was a sign of affection or the first signal of an underlying passive-aggressive anger. Or maybe passive-aggressive affection. The distinction was too subtle for him right now. He desperately needed caffeine to jump-start his mind.

That bite was not very passive, actually. He rubbed the spot on his neck and added another possibility onto the list: marking her territory.

He quickly recognized that these thoughts were too deep for him in his stimulant-deprived state. So he went back to remembering a few memorable scenes from last night's lovemaking.

Sally McLaughlin was the most inventive lover he'd ever experienced. She said that being paraplegic just meant that she had to turn her whole body into an erogenous zone. He didn't know about that, but he did know this girl knew her stuff!

He heard some hissing from another room. Then Sally wheeled back into the bedroom, now wearing a robe and carrying a tray with two croissants and two tall glasses of caffe latte.

She said, "The croissants are from Nabolom Bakery, but the latte's all mine. I practiced all afternoon with my new Jura-Capresso machine. I think I've got it down pretty good."

Speaking through a white mustache of foam, he said, "Perfect." He was already loving today!

Suddenly they were being serenaded by the "Dueling Banjos" theme from *Deliverance:* Sally's cell phone. This was the phone she used only for family matters. He knew she'd have to answer it. They had been waiting for a call from Heather, Sally's roommate and Warren's surrogate adolescent daughter. Heather had been up at Lake Tahoe for a ski trip when a big blizzard hit. They hadn't heard from her in two days. They were both more than a trifle worried.

Sally flipped open the phone and listened. Then she looked at him and shook her head. He guessed it wasn't Heather. Sally looked serious. Then she wheeled into the other room. Damn! He resented someone disturbing their morning together, but there wasn't much he could do about it. He took a dispirited bite out of his croissant and another sip from his rapidly cooling latte.

When Sally came back she still wasn't smiling, so he knew his day was heading straight for the trash can. "Warren, I have a big problem. I have a friend named Thérèse. You haven't met her yet. She lives in the city. She was the only friend who stayed with me after that Humvee cracked my spine. That was Vera on the phone. Vera's . . . ah, a close friend of Thérèse's. Actually, it's a little more complicated than that."

She paused, and took a breath. "Thérèse is a professional dominatrix and Vera is her personal slave. Very California. Anyway, Vera just told me that Thérèse was arrested for hanging one of her clients. I'm going to have to help her."

The taste of butter and crisp pastry turned rancid in his mouth. He was not quite tracking all this. After all, he was only halfway through his latte. But it sure didn't sound comforting. "You're going to help her. What's that mean?"

"That means I'm going to have to go to work right now. It also means I'd like your help."

Sally didn't ask for help. This was a big deal. And he knew that he should jump on the chance to help her. After all, she'd been there for him so often when he really needed her. True, sometimes she had helped as a paid consultant. But other times she had just jumped in free of charge. She was one fine woman.

If only *he* were a good person. Instead, he wanted to kill her. How dare she? This was supposed to be their luxurious, lazy morning, revisiting all those lovely positions they explored last night. Work was the last thing on his mind. Damn!

He so wanted to whine, to say, "I don't wanna help."

Luckily, he had better sense than to grovel in front of Sally. He knew that he had to be cool. Unloading his disappointment on her while she looked so obviously upset would not be very skillful. Plus he'd look like the jerk that he truly was.

But he'd be damned if he was going to get involved with yet another dead body and play detective for some whip-wielding pervert. Three times last year he'd been embroiled in murders. Twice he'd been the object of a police manhunt. Once his head nearly got blown off. All he needed now was a camcorder and he could be the next blockbuster reality-TV show. No, it was time for the drama to stop. He was retiring from the justice business.

"Look, Sally, I'm exhausted. Will you still care about me if I go back to being a tarot card reader? If it's all right with you, I don't want to get involved with helping out your friend." He couldn't read Sally's face. It looked neutral. Was she disappointed, annoyed, or didn't she care?

"I understand, Warren. You want your life to go back to normal. It's not going to reset, but I understand your desire to have that happen."

"What do you mean, it won't reset?"

"It has to do with Complexity Theory, and I don't think you're in the mood for a lecture right now. Finish your latte. I'm truly sorry. I know this morning wasn't supposed to go this way. Anyway, I am going to need to get to work, so I guess our date is over for now."

Dismissed ever so sweetly. He couldn't stand to watch her wheel away from him and over to her computer. *He leaped out of bed, viciously grabbed her chair, spun her around, and screamed into her face, "How could you do this to me?"*

OK, that was just his sick fantasy. It's what he wanted to do. But Sally owned an attack dog, so pissing her off was never a great idea. Instead, he meekly said, "Sally, wait just a sec before you go. Tell me what you meant when you said I can't go back to normal."

She turned her chair back toward him and sighed. "OK, I guess I owe you that. I tend to look at things more mathematically than you do, Warren. So bear with me as I try to translate.

"Here's how your life looks to me. Two years ago your life was orderly. Sure, you had your manic-depressive cycles, but they were more or less controlled by medication. You were a loner. You had your job reading tarot cards on Telegraph Avenue every weekend. You had your fixed schedule for every day of the week.

"Then came last year: all the murders, all the police attention. Your life became unpredictable. You have a bunch of what mathematicians call 'attraction points.' Some of them are: . . . ," she held up one finger at a time, "your old lifestyle of changing identities every few years or so, your fear of getting caught by the police, your feelings about me, your loyalty to Heather, all your emotions about becoming an instant father and grandfather."

She closed those five fingers into a fist. "What's worse, those attraction points have become 'strange.' That means they have become unpredictable; the points are always changing location and intensity. You can't tell what's going to happen next. Will I dump you? Will your daughter disown you? Will Tara start acting like your sister rather than your inquisitor? Is it your night to babysit your grandson? Will the police track you down? Will Heather come back from her ski trip?

"You just want to go back to your simple, predictable life again. And you're going to try to do that. But your life is now ruled by the laws of chaos and none of your old rules are going to work. So that's my math lesson for the day. Now, get out of here and let me work. I'll let you know if Heather calls."

Now he knew that he was really dismissed. He really hated today.

"OK. Maybe I'll be able to help you and your friend out after I feel more rested." He was lying. He had no intention of getting involved with this mess.

She wheeled over to her computer desk. "Keep imagining that you're in control of your own life, Warren. It's a comforting, if antiquated, notion." Then she started typing. No smile, no good-bye kiss, nothing.

He gave Ripley, her rottweiler service/guard/attack dog, a pat on the head. She licked his hand. At least that bitch was affectionate. Then he walked out of Sally's ranch house, shaking his head.

CHAPTER TWO

As Warren patted her dog, Sally almost opened her mouth to shout, *"Stellen!"* If she had done that, Ripley would have lunged at him and knocked him to the floor. Then her excellent dog would have leaped on his chest, bared her teeth, and dared him to make a move. It was just what the SOB deserved.

The Goddess Council stopped her. There were too many votes against the rebel goddess Venge's plan. Sally let Warren lope off unscathed. But it wasn't easy.

Sally always had voices inside her head. Well, really they were more than voices. It was like Sally lived in two worlds. One was what we call the normal world. Her name for that was the Prime Material Plane. The other land she inhabited was within her, a place she called Anthemion. A number of beings lived there, and several spoke to her regularly. By the time she was seven they were in constant conversation with her. She'd laughed when she read the research that "proved" that multitasking adversely affected performance. Hell, she couldn't decide what to have for breakfast without a lively debate. In rehab, she'd contemplated diagnosing herself with multiple personality disorder.

She almost told her therapist about the people inside her. But one of the voices stopped her. *Look, honey,* Psyche told Sally, *we all get along in here. We work together. Besides, you didn't come from a childhood where you were raped, beaten, or tortured. Not too much, anyway. You're not a multiple. But if you start telling some two-bit shrink about us, you're going to end up on Thorazine faster than you can chant* "Mēnin aeide thea."

These days there were usually only three folks in Anthemion who considered themselves her regular consultants. Psyche, wearing simple linen goddess-wear, was the therapist on Sally's council. As Warren walked out the door, Psyche was patiently listening to Venge rant. Venge, the rebel, had spiky short hair and always wore leather.

Right now Venge was on a rip about Warren. *Look, Sally, it's time to cut Warren loose. "Strange attraction points," my ass. He's a loser. He's a runner. Look at him walking away. There he goes, deserting you to go off and play his little "I'm a fugitive from the Weather Underground!" game. As if anyone cared. Men! We can't live with them, and it's against the law to castrate them. I say dump him.*

Psyche patiently observed, *Well, Warren has had a lot of trauma associated with all those murders last year. It's understandable that he might not want to plunge into another one.*

Old Spider Woman was rocking away in the corner. She was an elder at Anthemion, perhaps the oldest being living there. She was the spooky one. Most of the time all she did was rock. But all the other voices got silent whenever she spoke.

The last time she completely took charge was in rehab, after an Army Humvee had landed on top of Sally's spine. All the other voices had given up as Sally lay on her hospital bed, crippled and seriously contemplating suicide. Old Spider Woman stood up and said, *This must not happen. That joy-riding corporal who drove over your body must pay for his crime.* In that moment, Venge came riding up on some sort of cross between a Harley and a chariot and joined the council. With her attitude, suicide ceased to be an option.

This time Old Spider Woman said, *Venge is almost right. I agree with her. It's time Warren paid back his debt to you. Either make him help you, or cut him loose.*

But Sally would have to deal with all this later. The whole time this little inner scene was playing itself out, the part of her that worked in the Prime Material Plane had been on the Internet, laying down a virtual false trail into the San Francisco Police Department database.

She tried to stay away from law enforcement mainframes. After 9/11, the security had tightened up. She could still hack in, but she was worried about attracting Federal attention. This time she had no choice. All she could do was be careful.

If anyone tried to backtrack her entry, they would perceive this as a normal inquiry from the Santa Cruz Police Department. If they got past that, they'd end up at a feed store in the Midwest. After that, a public library in Seattle. No one but the best of the Feds could get any closer than that, and she had plenty of alarms set to warn her if that happened.

Now she was ready. The database opened up in front of her. Entering the name "Thérèse de Farge" gave her entry to the complete file on the murder. Scanning the medical examiner's report gave her a sour twist in her stomach. This really didn't look good.

CHAPTER THREE

The day was blown, anyway. Warren decided he might as well go to work. His office was on the corner of Telegraph and Haste, in Berkeley, California. Actually, his office *was* the corner of Telegraph and Haste. That's where he set up his waterproof cardboard table, his reinforced-steel folding chairs, and his Day-Glo sign that read: LOVE? SUCCESS? MONEY? YOUR ANSWER IS IN THE CARDS! DISCOVER THE TRUTH. TAROT CARD READINGS HERE.

Warren looked around and shook his head. April may be the cruelest month, but February was sure the coldest. Forget the sunshine fantasies of "California Dreaming"; this year the weather was better suited for *The March of the Penguins*. No snow, but a bitter, merciless wind. Mostly only weather-beaten locals were walking the street. No Botoxed suburbanite was going to make the hegira to the shrine of the counterculture on a day like this.

But locals were his stock-in-trade. And on a day like today, consulting the future might just keep you from cashing it in. Seasonal affective disorder was almost a prerequisite in this town. In Berkeley, eccentricity was conventional, psychopathology was de rigueur, and the only place you would find "normal" was on the dials of the washing machines in a Laundromat.

For those frozen masses yearning to be warm, Warren held out the hope for a future sunny day. He looked on his job as that of a poorly paid shrink, disguised as a prophet. He gave his marks (oops, *clients*) what they most needed: a false sense that there was some meaning to life in this unfeeling, erratic, chaotic universe. After a reading with him they were ready to go back out to the trenches. They left reassured that things would work out, if not exactly as they had planned, at least not as disastrously as they had feared.

There was only a handful of street merchants on Telegraph: a candle maker, selling various botanical organisms trapped in wax; a Rasta, hawking knitted tam-o'-shanters; a couple of jewelry stands pushing some shiny base-metal rings made in India and passed off as hand-crafted silver; a guy who would write your name on a grain of rice; and a stand of T-shirts proclaiming slogans like "Republicans—Over a Billion Whoppers Served," "Leave No Millionaire Behind," "The FBI Bugs Me," "Think Globally, Act Loco," and Warren's personal favorite: "Who Would Jesus Torture?"

He took another sip from his cardboard cup of espresso, and then sighed. The Ave looked like it was dying. It had one of those subtle wasting-away illnesses where you never know how bad the patient is until you're invited to the wake. The grocery had closed. Cody's bookstore had closed. Over twenty abandoned storefronts were staring with empty faces at a dirty, angry street. La Mèditerranée had new owners, and someone had stolen the regal high-backed chairs that used to look out at the street. A young Turk strode past Warren's table wearing a T-shirt that said: "Shut up, hippie!"

The mayor said all they needed to do was buy a street sweeper and get rid of the drug dealers and everything would be A-OK again. The mayor was deluded. Virulent cancer cells of despair were traveling through the veins of the street, eating away at the dream. Warren wondered how much longer he could last.

He took the final cold sip of his coffee. Perhaps the fault lay not in his streets but in himself. Warren knew a little about himself after almost four years of psychotherapy. Maybe it was his own psyche that was on the downward slide. This corner of California might have been a little drop of heaven, and he was just missing it.

He knew that he was not anywhere near normal, and he had the diagnosis to prove it. Even for Berkeley, he was fringe. He was a rapid-cycling bipolar. Rapid-cycling has nothing to do with Lance Armstrong. It means that whereas other people have mood swings, Warren had death and resurrection, sometimes only days or even hours apart. He was in good company: Virginia Woolf, Ernest Hemingway, Sylvia Plath, and other corpses. His present grimness might be a warning sign. He would have to keep his eye out for any fantasies about dramatically and tragically ending his vain and meaningless life. The conviction that this was the day to shuffle off these mortal coils was a clear indication that it was time to adjust his meds.

His first customer was a regular, Riva. She had finally crawled up the ranks of almost-unpaid teaching assistants to the poorly paid heights of an assistant professor of history. Seven more years of ass-kissing, and she might get tenure.

Riva had just submitted an article on the Sword of Destiny to some historical periodical and she wanted to know its chances of getting published. When he began to lay out the cards, the first out of the gate was the Hanged Man, which annoyed Warren greatly. Whenever there was a murder around, those pesky pieces of card stock started acting frisky. He told her to be patient, which is what the card signified. He didn't mention the hanged victim he was refusing to avenge.

It went on like that all day. Four cards haunted him. Death, the Hanged Man, Judgment, and the Tower kept frolicking through his readings: in pairs, triplets, and sometimes the whole quartet. He finally got sick of it and told his deck of cards to leave him alone.

Warren had an ambivalent relationship with his chosen profession. As a bomb-throwing member of the Weather Underground he'd missed a lot of the New Age, flower-power, Wicca, peace, love, and joy aspects of the sixties. For him the focus was more about taking down the running dogs of the capitalistic warmongers than basking in the Age of Aquarius. So he didn't believe in the hocus-pocus of tarot cards. His job reading them was just a benign con.

Unfortunately for him, the cards refused to be meaningless random events. They clumped, they bunched, and the ones he didn't want to see kept reappearing, especially when murder was in the air. The inexplicable behavior of these inanimate objects was very annoying, especially for the desperately rational side of himself.

He packed up his table, chairs, and sign and trudged down to the secret downtown parking place that only he knew about. For the thousandth time he thought, *When I get really poor, I'll sell its location for at least twenty thousand dollars on eBay.* Now, it was time to make his weary way home to his lonely apartment.

CHAPTER FOUR

S ally, I'm home!"

Sally clawed her way out of the San Francisco Police Department database, pulling herself away from field reports, autopsy records, scene-of-crime photographs. She shook her head when she realized that she hadn't heard either Ripley's barking or the house's Early Detection System going off. She'd been lost deep in virtual reality.

She called out, "I'm in here."

Heather Talbridge came bouncing into Sally's computer room. She couldn't help smiling. Here was a girl who, at sixteen, had been orphaned by the death of her father and the murder of her mother. She'd been kidnapped, drugged, and critically wounded. Yet her green-brown eyes still sparkled, her untamable russet hair framed her attractive face in an unruly halo, and she laughed like an innocent. Sally knew that Heather still had nightmares and gray, miserable weeks. But her spirit was getting feistier each month they lived together.

"God, Sally, I nearly turned into a Heathersicle! That was totally messed up!"

Sally restrained the impulse to lead off with, "Why didn't you call?" She was learning a little about how to manage an adolescent. Instead she said, "That was one hell of a storm. What happened?"

Heather peeled off her down jacket, dumped her wet pack in the middle of the floor, and petted Ripley, all the while unburdening a tale of spinouts, snowplows, dead cell batteries, and frigid cold. As bad as it probably was, by the time she was through with her narration it sounded ten thousand times worse.

Finally Heather flumped down in a chair next to Sally. "So wassup with you while I was gone? How's it going with Warren?"

"Warren who?"

"Uh-oh. Spill it."

"I either want to bounce this latte glass off of his head or want Ripley to give him a piece of my mind. And maybe take out a piece of his backside."

Heather leaned forward. "So why do you want to bean him?"

Back to reality, the cold reality of online data that she had been immersed in all morning. "Remember Thérèse?"

"Sure, your friend with the long hair and those great red nails. How is she?"

"In jail, for murder. And in deep. The cops have her fingerprints on the collar that strangled the 'vic,' who was a client of hers."

"Vic?"

"Oh, God, I've been reading field reports too long. Greg Hawkins, the man who died, was a victim of apparent sexual asphyxia."

"Ugh, gross. I've read about that. Guys hanging themselves and masturbating."

"Only Hawkins had his hands bound behind his back. That pretty well leaves out death by misadventure."

Heather cocked her head. "You said 'client.' What kind of client?"

Sally was quiet for a moment, wondering if she should bother to choose her words carefully. All the voices inside wanted to tell it straight. Heather was a friend, not a baby.

"Thérèse de Farge is a professional dominatrix. That quiet girl with the short blond hair that came over with her last month is Vera. Vera is her personal live-in, service-oriented submissive. That would translate as 'slave' to you. Vera called me this morning to tell me about Thérèse."

Heather hesitated. "Are you . . . is that something that you're into?"

"Well, I'd like to whip Warren's butt right now. But no, bondage and discipline isn't my thing. I was buds with Thérèse from high school."

"So why do you want to whip Warren's butt?"

Then Sally smiled. "And a very cute butt it is, I may say." The smile died. "I asked him to help out, but he went running back to Telegraph Avenue to play fortune-teller. Claimed he was tired out. Jeez, what's the matter with him? He's only been ripped off, beat up, run off the road, shot at, and nearly arrested last year. What a wimp."

Heather laughed. "Yeah, it has been the season of the witch for the poor guy, hasn't it?"

Sally went over to the window and looked out at the verdant hills behind her house. She was silent, trying to frame what she wanted to say. Finally she started wheeling toward the kitchen. "Come on, let's go get us something to eat. I'm famished. We'll talk while we eat."

Tuna sandwich prep went quickly, and soon they were seated in the sun.

"Twice, Thérèse saved my life. The first time was when I was ten. Thérèse—actually her name was Doris back then—stopped my dad from killing me.

"I don't think very many people get off with a free and easy childhood. Heather, I know yours was pretty messed up with the death of your dad. Not the same for me. If my dad had died it would have really improved my life as a kid. He drank, and he had a temper. We knew when to disappear. It was a necessary survival skill.

"One day—I was about ten—I had mumps. I was as sick as I had ever been. Dad came home in one of his drunken rages. . . ."

She'd heard him yelling from outside the house. At first she pulled her quilt over her head. Dad's hoarse screaming was more stimulus than she could handle. Her head was splitting open. She was roasting from the inside out. The left side of her face was swollen. Every time she tried to escape to the land within her, Anthemion, all she could hear was the sobbing of some unseen little girl.

The door boomed as he slammed it open.

"Where's my woman? Goddamn it, I want my dinner!"

He was in a wild drunk. The safest place for her was under the covers. But suddenly something snapped inside of her. It was probably the fever, but all she knew was that she had to silence her father. She crawled out of the bed, and nearly fell over as she tried to stand. *Easy, go easy.* She began to shiver, and wrapped her robe tightly around her. It was just a few steps to the door, and a few more to the top of the stairs. Then she would stop him from screaming. At the top of the stairs, holding tightly to the banister, she looked down.

"What the hell do you want?" He glared at her, eyes bloodshot, cheeks and nose red from the angry lava flowing inside him. Her dad was in that lethally dangerous place.

And Sally didn't care. She quietly realized that Dad killing her would be a blessing for everyone. She would no longer be in pain. He would go to jail for a very long time or, even better, get sent to the electric chair for murder. Whatever happened, the rest of the family could finally relax.

As loud as she could manage she said, "Shut up, you drunken bastard."

His eyes turned gray and empty. He began looking around for a weapon. Her brother's baseball mitt and bat were next to the front door. Perfect. He grabbed the bat and headed for the stairs. She waited, patient and resigned.

Just then, her best friend, Doris, came bursting through the front door. This was standard operating procedure for Doris, who hated to wait around for anyone to let her into a house. Dad had no idea she was there, so intent was he on homicide.

She took it all in, immediately. Both Doris's parents were drunks and drug addicts, so she wasn't that freaked out at this scene in front of her. She looked in the living room and saw what she needed. Far faster than Sally's dad could stumble up the stairs, Doris ran to the end table next to the couch and picked up a fat, round silver cigarette lighter. In one smooth motion she chucked it like a fastball right at Sally's father's head.

Sally heard the thunk as it smashed into his skull. He went down face-first on the stairs and started to roll.

Doris clasped her hands over her head. "Strike three, you're out! Come on, Sally. Let's drag him into the living room!"

Like in a dream, Sally carefully walked down the stairs, stepping cautiously around the sprawled body of her assailant. Together, but mostly using Doris's strength, they propped him into an armchair and placed a book in his lap. Then they turned on a reading light, and Doris followed Sally as she went back to bed, giggling as she tucked the quilt around Sally's pale shoulders.

Sally put down her half-eaten sandwich and sipped her Diet Coke. "Dad never said a word about it. I doubt that he even remembered it. He was in a blackout when he came at me. He probably always wondered where that knot on his skull came from. So I owe Thérèse a lot, maybe even my life.

"And then, when I was paralyzed after the army crushed my spine, she stood by me when everyone else got too uncomfortable to hang around with the cripple. Saved my life again, really. It's my turn now."

CHAPTER FIVE

The message was waiting for him as he walked into his Berkeley apartment. "Warren, this is Phillip. I'm temporarily residing at the U.C. med center, Oncology, room 233. I emphasize the word 'temporarily.' I would recommend that you visit me sometime very soon."

The hits just kept on coming. What was next? Warren drove to the city, expecting to get plastered by a meteor as he crossed the Bay Bridge. It was that kind of day.

Two things he'd learned about hospitals: One, it was a lot harder for them to brush off a live person than a voice on the phone. And two, family members rule. He had a feeling that time was of the essence. The charge nurse stopped him as he was striding past the desk.

"Can I help you?"

"Yes, please. My name is Warren Letour and I think you have my brother Phillip here?"

The nurse glanced down at his charts. Warren was doing his Obi-Wan mind-control thing: *These aren't the droids that you are looking for. You do not want to see any ID.* It worked. The nurse looked up and said, "Yes, Mr. Letour; it's room 223, the room at the end of the hall on the left-hand side."

Phillip looked like an animated corpse. His gigantic body rose under the sheet, a worn-down mountain range below his gray face. His eyes were ringed in dark circles as though someone had beaten him. Lines of pain stretched across his brow like razor wire, but he managed a smile of recognition.

"Ah, Warren. Good."

"Hello, Phillip. You look like hell."

"Headache. Like acid. Brain tumors aren't supposed to hurt. Bull!"

He closed his eyes and the lines on his face bit in even deeper. He groaned. Warren just stood there and waited. Time refused to pass.

Finally Phillip was back. He looked up. "Rough one. Big waves." He paused. "Oh, shit. Another one."

It was scary to watch the big man's mind devour him. "Can I call a nurse?"

Phillip barely managed to get out a no before he started groaning again. Warren pulled over a chair and sat down to wait.

Phillip forced his eyes open. He was panting now, short of breath from managing the pain. He pointed to a set of keys on the tray beside him. Between breaths he said, "They tell me . . . it might be operable. But they don't think my heart can make it . . . through the surgery. Need you to go to my apartment. Aluminum box plugged into the wall. The cards are there. Code is zero, one, two, three, five. Take care of them for me. Hold on. . . ."

Then he closed his eyes and slid back down into the pain.

In the silence, Warren thought back to when he met Phillip in Mexico, more than thirty years ago. Warren was down there setting up a new identity for himself. Phillip was reading tarot cards in a tiny candlelit shed. He'd told Warren exactly what fears were pursuing him. Warren had fled from Phillip as fast as he could.

When they met a second time, years later, Warren had become a tarot card reader on Telegraph Avenue in Berkeley. Phillip walked up to his table and in three minutes laid out Warren's choices: keep on the run for the rest of his life or dare to love someone.

They'd only met one other time. Again Phillip had stopped by Warren's table on the Ave. Phillip foretold the death of one of Warren's clients and the role he would play in delivering justice to the murderer. Phillip was scary, but Warren really didn't want the fat man to die.

Phillip's eyes opened. They were an even darker mahogany than usual. "Cards are seven hundred years old. The second deck ever painted. Someone wants them very badly."

Phillip gasped, then let out the deepest moan yet. He held his hands over his eyes and shook his head back and forth. His breathing became very labored and Warren got up to get someone. Phillip's weak voice stopped him at the door.

"Wait. Come back. No nurse. They'll put me under. Sit. I think I have some breathing room now. Let me tell you what I can about the cards.

"Sardaz, the painter of the major arcana cards, was a Sufi. Sufis hide Truth right out in the open. The cards are teaching aids. Flash cards for the soul. Handed down from teacher to student for six centuries. They affect each person differently. No idea what they will bring you. But find out about numbers. It's all about the numbers."

He had the wrong guy. "Wait a minute, Phillip. I don't know what you're talking about. What numbers? I don't deserve your cards. I'm not your student, and I'm sure no mystic. I mean, it's a great honor and all that, but—"

Phillip was gone, twisted back into his pain. Then his eyes opened very wide. He looked at Warren and said, "Oh, so it's like this." Then his giant body spasmed once and was completely still. No breath. All the alarms on the machinery around him went off. Warren yelled for help. A nurse ran in and then called something out down the hall. Warren grabbed the keys off the table.

He heard the Code Blue command as he walked away from Phillip's room. He passed the crash cart and the doctors running. He didn't think there was anything they could do for Phillip now.

On the ride from the hospital to Phillip's place, Warren was feeling sorry for himself. As well as very pissed off. Death and Misery had planted a thriving crop. Now Phillip was being harvested. He was getting tired of it.

Phillip's apartment was in a complex that clung to a hill overlooking Fisherman's Wharf. Thank God it was a relatively tourist-free Monday or he never would have found a parking space. As it was he had a short uphill hike. He walked across the patio and past one enormous wooden patio chair. The door opened to a small one-bedroom apartment. Bright light flooded in from the living room window overlooking Marina Green, Aquatic Park, and the sun glinting off the bay.

The room was like a hothouse. The big man must have really loved the Mexican climate, because his heater was jammed up as far as it could go. Warren was glad he had left the door ajar and now he opened a window to get some cross ventilation.

Phillip had a Zen-like approach to interior decorating. One huge leather chair, a small dining room table with one chair, walls Navaho white and bare. The door to the bedroom was open, and Warren could see a king-sized bed and more bare walls.

The only sound was a low hum coming from the one idiosyncratic touch in an apartment that was otherwise reminiscent of a monk's cell. Next to the leather chair was a furniture dolly. Strapped onto it was a metal box, about two feet square. A thick electric cord ran from the corner of the box to a three-pronged outlet in the wall. This must be the home of his new cards.

Before Warren could unplug the box, the phone rang. He let the machine pick up the message, but he could hear the caller clearly. The caller spoke in a tight, terse tone.

"Phillip, this is Troy. Please call me. I have a situation that is spiraling out of control and I need your help. I'm in town, and I need to see you. My cell is—"

Warren picked up the phone. This poor guy needed to know what had happened.

"Hello, Troy, my name's Warren and I'm a friend of Phillip's. I have some bad news for you. I'm afraid Phillip is in very critical condition. I'm sorry."

"Oh. I knew he was ill, but I didn't realize . . . Look, are you going to be at his apartment for a while?"

"Yeah?"

"Well, my name is Troy Baker, and I lent him an old used deck of tarot cards. I'm wondering if I can drop by and pick them up."

This slime bucket wanted to get his hands on Phillip's cards. "Actually I was just going out for lunch. But I should be back here around two o'clock. I can meet you here. Do you have the address?"

"Yes, of course. That's great, I'll meet you then. Thanks, Warren."

He knew that he had to move fast. He had a sense that Troy was flying across the city right now to get here and grab this box. God knew how big this guy was. Warren didn't want to go mano a mano right now.

He slammed and locked the window and unplugged the box. Then he wheeled the dolly outside, locking the door behind him. Breaking and entering might slow Troy down a little. Getting that box down the hill to his car was a battle with gravity. He had to dig in his heels to keep it from taking off down the steep slope.

There were two boards with guide rails on their outside edges strapped onto the handles of the dolly. When Warren got to his car he discovered their use. They were a portable loading ramp. This little unit weighed a couple of hundred pounds at least. He set up the rails and carefully started to guide the unit into the car, praying that it wouldn't tip over. His prayers were answered, and he got it safely ensconced on the backseat.

As he was pulling out, he noticed a beat-up brown Toyota Tercel slowly cruising down the hill toward him. Was this his new friend, Troy the rip-off artist? Only one way to find out. Start slow. Warren pulled out. Soon the other car joined the parade, letting two or three cars separate them.

Warren slowly wound through the city, watching his rearview

mirror. What an amazing coincidence! The Tercel seemed to match his route precisely. Doubting that this was just synchronicity, Warren prepared to ditch the guy.

Warren had always fantasized how he might shake a tail. Came from reading too many mysteries. This was his first opportunity to try out his plan. First he headed for Russian Hill, hoping to "go to ground."

He almost got caught in a dead-end trap on Chestnut, and yanked his wheel just in time to get on Grant. He was boxed in by a red Prius and a delivery truck from William's Fine Furniture. Warren hit his horn, twisted the wheel, and cut across the street. The car bounced onto the sidewalk and a young couple jumped out of the way screaming and giving him the finger.

He drove down the sidewalk toward a small street and then twisted the car down it, praying silently that it didn't come to a dead end. Blast, it did. Nope, just before the brick building at the end there was a small street heading off to his right. He saw the Tercel just starting to turn into view as he twisted down that alley.

It spilled out on Greenwich, which was blocked solid. He made a hard right and ended up in a tiny cul-de-sac, wedged in behind a Pacific Gas and Electric van. He sat there ten minutes hoping that he was invisible. Then he pulled out. No Tercel in sight. He started down Grant, feeling crafty like a fox. That's when he spotted his nemesis in the rearview mirror. OK, no more Mr. Nice Guy. This time was for keeps! He headed for the freeway.

He toodled across the Bay Bridge toward Oakland, choosing a middle lane and driving with the traffic. Troy was hanging three cars back. On the other side of the bay Warren put on his right turn signal, indicating that he was headed for downtown Oakland.

The lane he was in could go either right toward Oakland or

left toward Berkeley. A lot of lane switching happened in the last few hundred yards. A panel truck cut in front of Troy, trying to get to Berkeley at the last minute. Warren swerved to the left as soon as Troy's vision was blocked. The truck shielded Warren as he bounced over the warning bumps. He glanced up as he made the hard left onto Highway 80, and saw a blond head in a brown Tercel looking around frantically as Warren headed away from him into Berkeley.

His glow of triumph lasted until halfway up the second set of stairs to his third-story apartment. It was brutally hard work to haul this possibly two-hundred-pound dolly up stair by stair. By the time he was wheeling it down the hallway to his front door his arms were trembling. Make that three hundred pounds.

His place didn't have three-pronged plugs, but Warren had plenty of pigtail adapters. He plugged in the unit and it started humming, happy in its new home. Warren punched in Phillip's code, and heard the snick of the electronic lock. He opened the door.

A dark red wooden box was attached with tiny bungee cords to the only shelf in the safe. He opened the tarnished brass latch and lifted the lid. Inside the padded box was a red silk bag. He'd seen that bag before, the time Phillip had done the previous reading for Warren. He was afraid to touch the cards that he knew were inside it.

Sitting at his small, circular dining room table, he opened the bag and took out the cards. They had been carefully remounted on reinforced card stock to preserve them. The colors were surprisingly bright for their age. Gold predominated, but there were rich, dark indigos, vibrant yellows, and rich burgundies. Each image

34

filled the card. The background appeared flattened, as in medieval tapestries.

The suited cards were static and uninteresting. But the major arcana, the cards that Phillip said had come from the Sufi master, pulsated with energy and aliveness. They reminded Warren of the images he had seen of ancient Italian decks, but these were subtly different, more disturbing and more surrealistic than any deck he had seen. There was a glow in the eyes of the figures that had survived centuries of handling. It was almost as if they were regarding Warren, holding him against some unseen scale to see how he would measure up as their new owner.

And there was something else that really bothered him. A tingling in his hands, like the cards carried some tiny electrical charge from a minuscule inner battery.

He started to put them back in their bag. One fell out and landed facedown on the table. This had happened to him before. One card would almost jump out of the pack to inform him of some new monster slouching toward Berkeley to pounce on his life and devour it. He really didn't want to learn anything from these cards.

He really didn't want anything more out of life than to get bored at the bland sameness of a life without homicides to investigate and without punishment and retribution to deliver. For a moment he regretted not letting Troy walk away with the whole damn deck.

He put the other cards away in their red silk home. He sat still just looking at the back of the card that had dropped out. He knew that whatever transformative process these cards had in mind for him would begin when he turned over that card. He didn't want to touch it.

Sitting there paralyzed, he thought to himself, *I want a break. I just want my life to go back to the way it used to be. I want my little job on weekends on Telegraph Avenue. I want to find out if this girlfriend thing is going to work. Maybe to get to know my daughter a little better. That's all. No more felonies.*

He felt like hell. It was as though some overstressed buttress inside his belly was cracking and slowly giving way. And the roof, in slow motion, was falling down on him. Once again, his life was collapsing.

He turned over the card.

2
THE NUMBER TWO

TWO IS what cabalists called the "wisdom" number. One plus one makes two. When one reflects upon himself or herself, wisdom arises. Yes, much can be learned in meditation. But self-reflection is often not enough to achieve true knowledge. Two is the principle that reminds us we need other people if we are to grow, to succeed, and to understand. Asking for help and receiving it are manifestations of this energy. As Phillip would say, "That's why God created more than just one person."

CHAPTER SIX

Sally spoke intensely. "Thérèse, we *will* get you out of there. You have my word on it. I'm sending Clyde Berkowitz over to— Oh, you've got one already. Well, we are coming at this thing from a number of— OK, I'll let her know. Just hang in there, babe. We're out here working for you. . . . I have her number somewhere, I will call her. . . . Oh yeah, right. Don't worry, I'll take it out in trade. Now, shut up and sit tight. Bye, babe!"

Sally hung up and started opening drawers frantically.

"Vera, Vera, where are you?" Finally, she pulled out a battered brown address book. "Here's the little sucker!" She opened it and found the number she was looking for. Sally dialed and then tossed the book back into the drawer of chaos.

"Vera, it's Sally. Just talked to Thérèse. Get your little butt over here, we are having a strategy session. . . . I want you here five minutes ago. . . . OK, see you."

Sally looked up to see Heather looking at her with a wrinkled brow. Sally said, "Hey, I was kidding about taking it out in trade. Really, humiliation is not my thing."

"You have strange friends," was all Heather said.

"Yeah, strange roommates, too."

They both smiled, but before Heather could fire the next salvo, the phone rang. Sally picked up the cordless phone on her lap, looked at the screen, and spoke into her headset. "I told you that you'd be calling back. You just can't stay away from chaos, can you, Warren? . . . You bet, come on over. Bye."

Sally looked at Heather. "Something's wrong. I mean something else besides everything else that is wrong today. Warren's on his way over. He wouldn't say why, but he sounded strange."

Warren ran his fingers through his hair. Telling them the story of Phillip on his deathbed, he'd looked a little sick. He brightened up narrating the chase scene from San Francisco. Then he was silent for a while.

"And the card I turned over was, of course, the Hanged Man. In a lot of decks the guy hanging upside down has a peaceful expression on his face. In some decks the card is called the Acrobat and he looks like he's just about to perform some clever trick. Usually it's interpreted as indicating a time to be more reflective, since you aren't able to take effective action. The lesson is something about knowing that way down you are not in control of the Universe. All you can do is suit up, show up, and let the unfolding take care of the results.

"But in this deck the guy is upside down, his hands are bound, and he looks terrified. In medieval times, around the time this deck was painted, they used to hang traitors upside down and beat them until they died. That's the look on this guy's face. There wasn't anything serene about it.

"I'm not completely clueless. I can take a cosmic hint, especially when it clubs me over the head. I woke up this morning to hear about a hanged man—the guy your friend Thérèse is being framed for killing. Then the damn card chased me all day, showing up in my readings on the Ave. But when it fell on my table, that's when I knew there was no recess.

"Then the weirdest thing happened to me. I could feel the collar tightening around my neck. I couldn't breathe. And I panicked. In that instant I knew exactly what that guy felt as he was dying. Whoever or whatever was directing my life last year is back. And wants me in the middle of this, damn it all."

Sally reached out and touched his arm. "I'm really sorry about Phillip. You don't have a lot of mentorlike guys in your life besides him."

Warren looked out the window, slowly stroking Sally's dog, Ripley. No one said anything for a while. Finally Heather interrupted the tableau.

"So, where do we start?"

Sally wheeled her chair around and aimed it at Heather. "*We?* You're not getting anywhere near this mess. This is no place for a girl."

Heather gave her one of those I-never-realized-how-retarded-you-really-were stares and said, "I am an emancipated minor. I slept with my first man, a twenty-four-year-old camp counselor, when I was fourteen. I've been to porn sites that make your incarcerated friend look like Mother Teresa. Don't even go there, Sally. Now I repeat myself, where do we start?"

Sally started to respond: "Now listen here, young woman—"

"Don't you dare 'young woman' me! First of all, you're not my mom. Second, how are you going to feel if your best friend goes to prison because you refused the help that I offered you?"

Sally started to open her mouth. Then she closed it. She glared at Heather, then sighed. Inside her mind the vote of her inner council was unanimous against protectionism. "OK, you're in. But only if you do exactly what I want you to do."

Heather grinned. "Trust me."

"Yeah, right." Sally turned her chair to face Warren. Before she could speak, Ripley began barking. Then a red light began flashing, and a soft gong began to chime. The large TV screen in the living room flickered on and showed a petite blond woman coming through the front gate.

"That's Vera." Both Sally and Heather spoke at the same time. Sally gave Ripley a command in Dutch, and she stopped barking and sat quietly next to Sally. Heather opened the door. Vera gave her a quick hug without smiling and started toward Sally. When she spotted Warren she stopped dead. "Who's that?"

Sally said, "Warren Ritter, meet Vera— I don't know your last name."

"I don't have one. 'Vera' is fine." She crossed her arms, still looking warily at Warren.

Sally went on, "Warren caught three murderers last year. He's here to help us out."

Vera turned to face him straight on. "Are you a private eye?"

"No, I'm a tarot card reader."

Vera uncrossed her arms. "Oh, wow. Did you use the cards to solve the murders?"

"Sort of."

"That's very cool. I'd like to talk with you sometime about how you do that. I read the cards, too, but I'm no professional."

Sally cut in, "OK, chat time later. Right now we've got to figure a way to get Thérèse out of jail. Come on over to the table, everybody, and let's get started. The best way to help Thérèse is to find out who really killed this guy, ASAP. Vera, why don't you start? Tell us what you know."

After everyone got settled, Vera took a big breath and sighed. Then she began.

"I can't tell you much. Thérèse got home late last night. It was a long day. She serviced four clients, which is a lot more than she usually does. I had her dinner ready and gave her a massage after that. We went to bed sometime past midnight. This morning there was a knock at the door. When I answered it, two policemen and a policewoman were outside. They told me they had to see Thérèse about one of her clients. When she finally came down, they arrested her and took her off. That's when I called you. Thérèse called me from jail and told me to come over here. That's all I know."

Sally looked down at her yellow pad of paper. "Here is why they showed up at your front door, Vera. At 7:07 P.M. a George Walker called the SFPD. He lives in a loft south of Market. He had been walking from the elevator to his unit when he passed an open door. He glanced in and saw a dead man. Police found that the victim, Greg Hawkins, was tied to a pole and handcuffed. He was wearing a collar pulled tight enough to cut off all air. There were some fingerprints on the latex. When they ran a check, Thérèse popped up as a match. She had a prostitution prior that put her prints in the criminal database. It's all circumstantial so far, but it looks pretty bad."

Vera put her head in her hands and began to sob. Sally asked, "What's going on, girl?"

"Thérèse did outcall scenes for that guy in his loft. She told me about him. He runs a big computer security company. He had an apartment all set up just to do those scenes. I'm sure they'll be able to find witnesses who have seen her there before. I don't know, maybe she was there yesterday. What are we going to do?"

Sally wheeled over to Vera's side and took her chin in her strong right hand. It was a gesture of domination. Vera immediately stopped crying and looked into Sally's eyes. Sally said, "No weeping, no weakness. That's not what Thérèse needs right now. Now tell us who might hate Thérèse enough to set her up for murder?"

As Vera began to speak, Sally let go of her face but held intense eye contact. "Well, hell, Thérèse was a dom. Everybody in the B and D scene either liked her or despised her. That's life as a dominatrix. But I think there was really only one person who detested her. That would be Steele. It's hated her for as long as I've known Thérèse."

Warren asked, "It?"

"Yeah, no one knows Steele's gender. Steele wants to be called 'it,' and people usually do what Steele wants. Anyway, it and Thérèse were in a bitter rivalry. Thérèse never told me why, but it must have been something really bad, because I never saw her angrier than she was when she had to deal with Steele."

A quiet descended. Sally leaned back in her chair, deep in thought. No one wanted to disturb her.

Old Spider Woman, Anthenium elder (still rocking): *This spiraling, twisting pattern has two arms. They weave together like the two sugar-*

phosphate backbones of a DNA molecule. One backbone twists around Thérèse, the other around Greg Hawkins, the victim. Follow their coiled path and you'll descend to the real killer.

"How can we get closer to Steele?" Sally asked.

Vera gave a tiny shake of her head. "Well, you could go to school with it. Steele runs the Academy of Correction, a training center for masters, mistresses, and professional doms."

Heather said, "Cool. I'd be into—"

Sally cut her off. "Don't even go there. You're not *that* emancipated. Besides, you're still seventeen: underage jailbait for a charge of contributing to the delinquency of a minor. Steele wouldn't touch you with a ten-foot whip." Then she looked over to Warren. "But you, on the other hand, would be a perfect candidate."

Warren sat up and shoved his chair away from the table. "Hey, hold on. I'm a lover, not a fighter. I don't even swat flies."

Sally wasn't impressed. "Nothing personal, honey, but you are totally full of it. You are an eccentrically dangerous person. You just haven't plumbed the depth of your true sadistic nature. What a learning opportunity this is going to be for you."

"No thanks."

Sally glared at him. "Look, Warren, Steele is our number-one suspect right now. The cops think they have their killer. They're not going to worry about tracking down anyone else. The only people that give a damn about saving Thérèse's ass are sitting at this table. I'd do Steele's course in a minute. But the highest and best use of me is online, tracking down information about the late Mr. Hawkins. Steele sure isn't going to trust Vera. So that leaves you, Master Ritter."

Warren was the first to break away from the staring war that was going on between him and Sally. He said, "But I don't know squat about S and M. Steele would know I'm a phony in a minute."

Sally grinned. "Vera, how fast can you train Warren to pass as a wimpy top who needs more training?"

Vera smiled back, the first time she'd smiled all day. "Oh, depends on how apt a student he is. But I think I could get him whipped into shape in a one-day crash course. It's not going to take all that much training. Word on the street is that Steele is desperate for students for its new session. It has been out trolling for anyone with an opposable thumb, a flail, and a credit card."

Warren mumbled, "Fine. Do me."

CHAPTER SEVEN

Vera asked, "Warren, do you know what a 'top' is?"

"A spinning toy?"

She sighed. "We have a lot of work ahead of us. Lesson one: The top is the dominant partner and the bottom receives the discipline."

The cold spell had snapped like a suspender. Winter? What's that? Today: blue sky, gentle zephyr wind, and joy unconfined. This was the kind of day that inspired Tony Bennett to misplace his heart on that little cable car. Vera lived in the top flat of a Victorian in the outer Richmond District, an area usually barraged by on-shore winds and cold, merciless fog. But today the gold dome of the Russian Orthodox church was a glittering promise of redemption.

It was a perfect day to go to Ocean Beach and watch the surfers get swept out to sea in the riptide. Instead Warren was trapped in his new classroom, incurring the exasperation of his less-than-patient tutor.

Vera had a ballerina's body: tiny, tight, and graceful. Her yellow hair was in a short pageboy. It lit up like a halo in sunlight streaming in from the window behind her. She had on a gauzy summer shift in pastel lavender. Her most striking features were her deep, royal blue eyes. They were focused intently on him right now.

"OK, Warren, it's obviously too soon to be focusing on vocabulary tests. Let's start somewhere a little more fundamental. What comes into your mind when you think about bondage and discipline?"

"Controlled violence? Consensual rape? That joke about the masochist saying, 'Whip me!' and the sadist saying, 'No.'"

Another sigh. "'Consensual rape' is an oxymoron. But, in a weird way, you're on the right track. Bondage and discipline is an erotic consensual exchange of power. In vanilla sex (that's the kind you have) the main focus is on the exchange of sensual pleasure. That's fun, in a very safe, controlled, comfortable, and slightly boring way. Comparing that to BDSM is a little like equating making waves in a bathtub to surfing the Banzai Pipeline.

"What's missing in vanilla sex are the elements of power and danger. The top (who you called the sadist in your little joke) must reach inside and access within herself or himself a fountain of intensity, creativity, authority, dominance, empathy, menace, and extreme safety-consciousness.

"The bottom must call forth surrender, openness, compliance, and a willingness to give over control to someone else. Both parties must have the deepest respect for each other and, in an intense scene, both parties are ripped open to a passionate vulnerability."

He realized two things. One, Vera was a lot smarter than he'd given her credit for, and two, he didn't know beans about this form of sex. It frightened and enticed him. No, more precisely, *Vera* frightened and enticed him.

She walked over to the small couch he was sitting on and perched next to him, her thigh touching his. She said, "We can get to flail-management and knot-tying later. But first you've got to really sense into the power of this kind of intimacy.

"The first thing we do in any scene is design our alliance. I need to tell you the level of pain I am interested in tolerating, and any special rules I need you to respect.

"So here goes: Today, I need our play to exclude intercourse. Mild bruising is usually OK, but you may need to hold back a little until you find an effective level of pain delivery. I never want scenes that may lead to scarring or bleeding. Do you understand all the things I just told you?"

"Yes, I think so."

"OK. Our next order of business is to agree on 'safe words.' If I say 'green,' that means I'd like you to do whatever you are doing even more. If I say 'orange,' that means back down on the level of pain or fear you are generating. If I say 'red!' that means 'Stop right now! This scene is over. Untie me, or back off. I'm overwhelmed and I've had enough!' If you ever disregard my safe words, even for a moment, I will never play with you again. Understood?"

"Understood."

She placed her hand on top of his open palm and said, "Now, hurt me."

CHAPTER EIGHT

Heather quietly spoke. "OK, Boss Lady, I'm ready. Who do you want me to investigate?"

Sally turned away from her monitor and was shocked. Heather stood there wearing a beige pantsuit and a cream-colored blouse, sporting an emerald green scarf around her neck and very sensible heels. With her makeup and her hair in a French twist she looked ten years older. "Wow, you're Little Miss Corporate. I'm impressed."

"Well, I figured if I was going to dig around downtown I'd better chameleon myself."

"Oh, is that where you're going?"

Heather put her fists on her hips. "Yes. Look, you already agreed to make me a part of the team. Besides, what can possibly happen to me in the Financial District? Now give me a list of the late Mr. Hawkins's business associates and let me loose!"

"Who's the Boss Lady here?" But Sally was already tapping the keys on her keyboard and the printer began making noises. Sally went on, "OK, Hawkins owned Hawkins Computer Defense

Systems, a company that specialized in making corporate networks hack-proof. He's worth a bundle. I have a list of his major clients and chief competitors. Have you figured out how you're going to get in to talk to these folks?"

"Warren made me a press ID and some business cards for *Business West Coast Weekly.* I thought I'd tell them I was doing an article on the Hawkins empire. He also gave me a whole bag of really cool stuff to use to spy on people."

"I'm going to kill that man. Look, Heather, leave your little black bag at home. You may be interviewing a ruthless murderer. Do nothing to arouse suspicion, understand?"

"Aye, aye, Captain."

"And don't be a smart-ass. Now, I'll hack into the files of *Business West Coast Weekly* and put you on their list of stringers, in case anyone checks. Here are the names of the five closest competitors to Hawkins. Tonight, you can let me know how your first day as a PI went. And for God's sake, call me right away if anything feels even a little dangerous."

Sally watched Heather stride out of the house, a shiny brown leather briefcase tucked under her arm. She thought, *There goes a whole lot of initiative and resourcefulness.* This might be as close as she would get to motherhood, and she was proud of that girl.

Sally turned her attention back to her monitor. It took her ten minutes to get "Heather Talbridge" added to the roster of independent journalists affiliated with *Business West Coast Weekly.* Sally shook her head in contempt at any company that gave an outsider an infinite number of tries to log in to their intranet. She took out a two-year subscription while she was there, and charged it off to the National Right to Work Committee, a right-wing anti-union lobby. It still amused her to tweak the system.

Then it was back to the real work, attempting to penetrate HawkinsCDS.com. This system was state of the art. It demanded all Sally's energy. The Goddess Council stayed silent.

Sally first routed her input through an entry point in Hayden Lake, Idaho, and then to a mainframe she rented in Argentina. From that computer she put up a Guards and Wards program. It would disconnect her at the first sign that someone was backtracking her messages to South America. Then she went through a big unprotected portal at Walt Thomas's Feed and Tack. Most folks who were trying to tail her would get stopped here. No bread crumbs.

Then she attacked the Hawkins Computer Defense Systems site. It took her half an hour to get past the public pages to find the entry into the in-house intranet. It took her three hours to get into the company-wide site. Then she hit the entry page to the high-security section. Nothing she tried could get her past that damn log-in page.

Finally she attempted an all-out denial-of-service shotgun attack. This was a high-risk tactic, sure to get someone's attention. She only hoped she could get in and out before someone came after her.

She launched a program that would attempt to overwhelm the central processor with incoming messages both from the public Internet and from the in-house intranet. At the same time, she was coming at the protective ice that was keeping her out of the restricted area. Sometimes so much imput could initiate a fail-safe program that opened up an emergency access. If she could catch the hole as it opened she might be able to get in.

Two minutes into the attack she was bounced into a new screen, saying "Systems Coordinator Access." Then she was suddenly logged off the Internet. Uh-oh, they were coming after her while she was going after them. Someone had followed her trail back to Argentina and activated her protection program. The Hawkins security programming was as good as any she had encountered. She would need to come at this system through another route.

She decided to clear her e-mail and call it a day. As she was reading a few old messages, a new one downloaded.

Again, she was immediately logged off the Internet. The Guards and Wards program that protected her home site had just kicked in. This was not good! Someone had tracked her to the United States. That had never happened before.

She read the e-mail that had come in just before she was kicked off:

```
From: LH@HawkinsCDS.com
To: Ripleysprovider@earthlink.net
Subject: Congratulations!


Your security was almost as good as ours. You got
into a level no other hacker has ever penetrated.
Our company has three options at this point.
   One, we can try to take down your system. We
have been examining your security while you've
been probing ours. We decided that you might be
able to survive an all-out attack. A draw would
serve no one.
   Two, we could track down the physical location
of your mainframe and arrange an accident. But that
```

is only a temporary solution. As we both know, hardware is expendable.

Finally comes option three. We would like to interview you for a position in our company. Anyone of your skill level would be a great asset to us. You might just be interested in the offer of a very lucrative salary for doing what you currently do just for the challenge of it.

Sincerely,

Laura Hawkins, COO

P.S. Our team was very impressed with your security. It took us an hour to get around the Argentine entry point and we still can't pin down your physical location any more precisely than somewhere in northern California. Your protective systems are excellent! We'd love to make you an offer on some of those programs. Come by my office at 2:00 P.M. tomorrow if you are interested.

Sally laughed. She had been bested at her own game. How did they get around her warning program without triggering an alarm? She would definitely give Ms. Laura a call.

3

THE NUMBER THREE

IN ANCIENT traditions Three is the principle of exploration into the deepest reaches of the manifest world. Probing, studying, and never-ending investigating of the known world are all activities that Three embodies. It is the belief that through this kind of inquiry we can come to know the truth. And discovering the truth can become an obsession for some people.

CHAPTER NINE

Vera said, "It's time you got a look at the scene."

It had been a long and exhausting day. If Warren never flogged another butt it would be too soon. His palms stung from spanking. His fingers hurt from tying bowlines, surgeon knots, and rope handcuffs. His forearm ached from flailing. And he was tired of doing something for hours that he was obviously incompetent at.

The day alternated between hands-on experience, monologues about sadism and spirituality, and stern safety lectures, like:

"Prepare for every play session with three contingencies in mind: One, what will happen to your bottom if you become injured or otherwise incapacitated? Two, what will happen to your bottom in the case of an external emergency, like a fire, power failure, or earthquake? Three, what will happen if your bottom stops communicating with you? If you are not prepared to make this a safe scene you are not ready to be a top."

He'd asked about whips and Vera just stared at him. Then she said, "In a couple of years, maybe. A whip in the hand of a newbie is an invitation to the emergency room." OK.

He wanted to go home tonight and nurse a White Russian in the quiet of his living room. But Vera was just warming up. She was one controlling submissive, that's for sure.

"Here's your homework. Go out and pull together a wardrobe and meet me back here around ten. I want to take you to the Power Room, a play spot for BDSM wannabes like you."

"Hey, Vera, I didn't pick this job. Nice, normal, heterosexual lovemaking was good enough for me."

"Ten o'clock. And don't drink. I need you very sober!"

Where does one go to get a Torquemada costume? Warren refused to settle for some black chaps and a vest from a leather shop in the Castro. If he was going to be in this scene it would be his way. He headed out to the Haight, and to his favorite vintage clothing shop: Wasteland.

Haight-Ashbury was the spiritual home of the hippie movement. Today it was like Berkeley without the politics: lots of small head shops, pagan supply centers, bookstores, restaurants, and thrift stores. It hadn't been Disneyized, but it was very tourist oriented. Buses of Japanese sightseers came driving down Haight to see what those quaint freaks from the sixties looked like.

These days they don't see hippies. They see the homeless, hanging out with their kids and their dogs, waiting for something to happen. From the comfort of air-conditioned Land Cruisers, the visitors shoot their cameras at the picturesque scene.

The street facade of Wasteland looked like a bad acid dream, but inside was a warehouse of wonderful all-cotton Hawaiian shirts, leisure suits, skinny ties, polyester bowling shirts, denim, pearl-buttoned cowboy wear, motorcycle jackets, cardigans, and racks of dresses, all of which were of no interest to him. At least this undercover operation didn't involve cross-dressing.

Back in a pile of new arrivals he found exactly what he needed, merit badges and all. Tracking down a matching pair of poplin khaki Bermuda shorts was easy. Across the street at La Rosa Vintage he liberated an orange "Big Horn Training Conference" neckerchief, the perfect accent. A slide made out of a large galvanized hex nut from Roberts Hardware finished the job. He was ready.

Vera laughed. Warren thought he looked quite authoritarian in his scoutmaster uniform. She said, "Steele's going to love you. You've got just the right imagination for this job! OK, Fearless Leader, let's book."

There are places below Market Street in San Francisco where the city has just given up hope. Not Yerba Buena, where they leveled the tenements to build convention centers and tech museums. Not South Beach, with its fancy ballpark. But move toward Sixth and you get blocks of apartment buildings that rent by the week, tattoo parlors, pawnshops, and more homeless, addicted, alcoholic lost souls per square foot than in any other city in the United States.

Plunked down in the middle of this unnamed ring of hell was a square box with no windows and a discreet sign over the one door announcing THE POWER ROOM. The door opened to an NFL halfback dressed in black.

"Hi, Vera. What are you doing here?"

61

"Hi, Wayne. I'm here on business. Haven't seen you at Mission Control lately."

"I know, since I got this gig I've been working my butt off. Frank and I are trying to buy a place out in the Sunset."

"Good luck. What's admission these days?"

"Go on in, girl. It's on the house tonight. Hey, I'm sorry about Thérèse. How you doing?"

"Later."

"Who's your friend?"

"Forget about it, Wayne. He's straight."

"What a waste!"

As they walked up a set of stairs he could sense Wayne checking out his rear carriage.

They entered a place that looked a little like a western saloon, with a long bar and couches scattered about. The barkeep was putting up Calistoga water and Jamba Juice, since this was an alcohol-free establishment. Vera stopped to check her cape and then headed for the stairs.

They descended, coming out into a cavernous bazaar of the bizarre. A huge barred jail cell dominated the center of the room. Inside it, a woman was locked into a set of stocks right out of Salem. Another woman was administering repeated strokes of a flail to her bare backside.

Off to the right, in a huge oak four-poster, two couples were banging away on each other with good old-fashioned sex. Porno videos were going on in a chamber to the left, and live porno was being performed on the couch in front of the screen.

Farther into the room he could see an empty operating theater, the shiny metal stirrups silently calling for a volunteer. Vera was dragging him toward the rear of Market de Sade. There in the corner was a torture chamber that must have been used by the Inquisition. Flails, canes, chains, ropes, leather straps, handcuffs, leg irons, and all manner of whips hung from cast-iron racks attached to the stone walls. It was probably a very exciting landscape to a sadist, but the place looked seedy to Warren and somehow made him a little sad. He looked closer at some of the scenes.

A woman was bound in chains to a black metal column. She was blindfolded. A tall rail of a man, in black leather, of course, was attaching clips to her nipples.

A man was hanging on a large A-frame structure while a gal in high heels and the tightest corset Warren had ever seen was placing a latex hood over his head.

Another man in a tiny leather codpiece with a leather gag in his mouth was completely suspended off the ground in a leather sling while a burly gentleman caned his red bottom.

There was an eerie silence as each pair fiercely concentrated on the actions they were involved in. This was a high-intensity sport!

Vera whispered to him, "Pay close attention to the doms. Watch how the good ones keep their submissives safe. They are completely tuned into the level of pain they are delivering."

The woman in chains said something in a low voice. The tall man took the clip off her breast and bent close to her face to talk with her. Then he took off her blindfold and unwound the chains that held her to the column. She put her arms around him and collapsed. He carried her over to a dark blue velvet couch. He sat with her and just held her silently. For the first time since Warren had walked into the place he felt embarrassed. Sadism was unnerving, but this intimacy was even harder to witness.

Vera's grip on his arm tightened. "What's it doing here?"

He knew she must be referring to Steele by her choice of pronoun. He turned and saw a person of medium height standing behind them on the stairway, surveying the scene below.

"Its" gray hair was pulled back into a ponytail. Steele had a patrician face, high cheekbones, thin lips, and a long neck. It stood erect with the posture of an honor guard. It was wearing a fawn brown leather outfit, vest and pants that looked tattooed on. It was somewhere in its forties. If Steele was a man, he had very small private parts. If it was a woman, she had very small breasts. But either way the arms, crossed in front of its chest, looked sinewy and strong.

The person gestured toward Vera, indicating that it wanted her to approach. She began moving, almost involuntarily. Warren could sense Steele's commanding charisma.

"Who's this old hawk?" Steele gestured toward Warren.

Vera answered, "A friend of mine from way back, but he's new to the scene."

It dismissed Warren, looking back at her. "I heard about Thérèse."

Vera flashed, "You hate her anyway. Why do you care?"

"I didn't say I cared. I said I heard. I think it is time for the two of you to leave." It began to walk past them.

Vera actually started up the stairs. Boy, once a submissive, always a submissive. That kind of arrogant authority pissed Warren off. He just wasn't cut out to be a loyal subject. He grabbed her arm to stop her and turned to face Steele. "You're not my master. I'm not going anywhere. I'm just starting to like it here. My name is Warren, and yours is Steele, although you haven't seen fit to introduce yourself. I'm not very pleased to meet you."

Steele smiled, and looked at Warren's uniform. Then it said, "I was wondering if you had a voice."

Warren replied, "I was wondering if you had any manners."

"Not a strong suit for me, I'm afraid. Or for you either, apparently. I like your cockiness, old man." Steele reached into a vest pocket and pulled out a card. "Call me if you are interested in learning anything more than tying Boy Scout knots."

Warren looked down at the card. All it said was STEELE, THE ACADEMY OF CORRECTION and listed a phone number. When he looked back up, it was striding across the floor, heading toward the dungeon. Nice pert butt, but it walked like a man.

CHAPTER TEN

The train doors closed. Heather carefully studied her fellow passengers on the BART commuter train, looking for clues on how young people acted. She had to pass for straight, and needed all the help she could get. As she watched Miss Tweed entering material into her BlackBerry, Heather's thumbs twitched in mimicry. "It won't really matter what I type, just as long as I look like I know what I'm doing," she reminded herself.

Mr. Gray Double-Breasted next to her had his laptop strapped into his briefcase, so he could just flip open the cover and start typing. Tonight she would duplicate that system.

Today was probably just managing the administrative assistants, receptionists, and, if she was lucky, maybe an executive administrator or two that she'd have to speak to. What if she blew it? What if her fake IDs didn't work? Suppose they actually called *Business West Coast Weekly* for verification? She would be royally messed up!

The jerk of the train broke her anxious reverie, and she got up to join the herd piling out at the Montgomery Street station. She was looking at the legs of the woman in front of her. OK, tomorrow she needed a shorter skirt, higher heels, and sheerer nylons. Might as well make use of what she had in the way of eye candy appeal. She was sure most of the people she would be meeting would be geek guys, and a fine-looking babe might inspire them to go ahead with the interview without checking references. Whatever works!

By the time she got on the down escalator at six that evening the stiletto heels idea was history. Sneakers, maybe. She couldn't decide which muscles hurt more: calf, shoulder, or smile. Salespeople had to do this every day! She sat down, leaned back against the plastic seat, and closed her eyes, as the train raced into the tunnel under the bay.

"I will never rudely hang up on a telephone solicitor again. I will never tell off a pushy retail clerk again. I will never slam the door in the face of a real estate salesperson again." She whispered this catechism as she swayed from side to side with the rocking of the train.

She hadn't ever considered what it took each of those people to step into her world and try to sell her something. Now she knew the fear that comes right outside the door, as she prepared her speech and cranked up her cheerful energy. Now she knew the self-management it took not to just run away from the first no. Now she knew what it took to hold her ground and ask, "Well, when might it be convenient?"

And salespeople had to do this day after day, week after week, just to put food on the table. What raw courage! She was coming home with a seventeen-year-old humility in the face of the strength of her fellow passengers.

CHAPTER ELEVEN

S ally's exit was blocked by an indignant teenager. "You
aren't going anywhere in those clothes. They're totally Fart City!"

"Get out of my way. This is what I wear." Sally
bumped her chair into Heather's legs.

Heather wasn't budging. "You are *so* eighties! This isn't some
pizza feed with the geeks down at HackandSlash dot-com. This is
Corporate. I know! I was walking that beat all day yesterday. Levi's
and tees don't cut it anymore. Look, I don't know squat about
hacking. But clothes: That I know. And your Goodwill outfit won't
get you past the security guard. Good thing we're about the same
size. Follow me back to my closet and let's see what we can string
together. Sally, this is a non-negotiable demand!"

With Ripley trotting along by her side, Sally wheeled down the
street toward the forty-eight-story cylindrical glass tower of 101
California. She was wearing a navy suit with a red scarf cunningly

pinned in place by a gold-and-diamond brooch in the shape of a crescent moon. She felt like a mannequin from Ann Taylor, which was exactly what Heather had intended.

Hawkins Computer Defense Systems owned the thirty-fourth floor of the building, rubbing shoulders with Morgan Stanley and Merrill Lynch. Sally was impressed. That was one hell of a lease payment.

The elevator opened up to a lobby and one closed door behind the long-legged twentysomething receptionist. No one was going to be idly wandering around these hallways without getting past the gatekeeper. Sally wheeled into the lobby. The redhead looked uncertainly at Ripley.

Sally gave the receptionist her name and explained, "She's a service dog. Perfectly harmless. She goes everywhere with me. If you have a problem with that you might want to check the Americans with Disabilities Act Federal Regulation Code 28, Section 32.032 (c)."

The receptionist gulped and reached under her desk. The door clicked and automatically opened. "Go all the way to the end and it's the last door on your right. Have a nice day."

At the end of the hall on Sally's left was a wooden door with a brass name plate reading: GREG HAWKINS, CHIEF EXECUTIVE OFFICER. The door on the right was identical except that the plaque read: LAURA HAWKINS, OPERATIONS. Sally recognized the type of door as she opened it. It had a mahogany veneer over a level-seven bullet-resistant, steel-clad core. The same as she used in her house. Damn hard to break through, unless you were in an armored vehicle.

Another watchdog was guarding another door. This time it was a blond guy with a crew cut, Ben Franklin glasses, and big shoulders.

He was intently typing. He looked up and said, "Oh, hello. Do you have an appointment?"

"I'm here to talk with Laura Hawkins at two."

"Good. May I see some identification?"

"No."

That stopped him for a moment. But not for long. "OK. Let me check with her."

"That won't be necessary. Please come in." The door to the inner sanctum had opened and a tall brunette came over to shake Sally's hand. She was thin as a stick: all angles and points, with anorexic *Vogue* cheekbones and shiny olive eyes. The voice was contralto, the blazer was some luscious brown fabric with whipstitched piping, and the pants were slightly belled. Yves Saint Laurent does the sixties. Sally was glad she wasn't still in blue jeans. Even with Heather's help, she felt more outlet store than couturier.

"I'm Laura Hawkins. How do you do?"

Sally took her hand with a firm grip. "I do fine, thank you." Laura's handshake was every bit as strong as Sally's, which surprised her. Laura was no wimp.

"Please come in and let's talk."

Laura's beach-boy assistant spoke up. "The dog can stay here if you like."

Sally narrowed her eyes. "I don't like. The dog stays with me." Laura nodded her OK and Pretty Boy settled down. She held the door as Sally wheeled into the office.

Inside, a stream of water washed down a slate surface, making a sweet, restful murmur. One wall was all window, looking across the docks of the Embarcadero to the glittering bay. A tall, healthy ficus dominated one corner of the room. The furniture was yellow

71

butter-leather and the cherry desk had lots of technology built into it. Illuminated behind the desk was an oil painting of a gnarled gray tree, red fields, and threatening clouds. It looked suspiciously like a Vlaminck. A vast, thick Persian rug in burgundies, ambers, and midnight black made traveling difficult for Sally. She wheeled in front of the desk and waited.

Laura glided over and perched on the corner of the desk. "You are quite a mystery. We still can't seem to get any closer to your true location, and we have no idea as to your identity. Considering the resources we have devoted to those two tasks, I hold you in the highest respect."

Sally knew she was being manipulated. She was determined not to show how much she liked it. "How did you keep my alarms from going off?"

"Oh, they went off. We just managed to route the packets to our server instead of to yours."

All the original oil paintings in the world couldn't make a bigger impact on Sally than this simple statement. She would give her eyeteeth for a program that could strip the addresses off packets and bond on new ones.

Laura's computer beeped, and she got off the edge of the table to look at the screen recessed into her desk. She looked up. "May I call you Sally?"

Sally smiled. She was not about to be one-upped. "Visual recognition program linked into the DMV, using the images from your surveillance cameras. Very neat. I know a lot about you, too. I'm sorry about the accident when you were sixteen, but the surgeons did an excellent job. Better than new."

Laura's turn to smile. "We sound like a couple of guys trying to outdo each other over the size of their privates. We're both good at what we do. I don't want to compete with you. I want to hire you."

Sally listened to Venge's warning to play hard-to-get. "Why should I work for you, or for anyone, for that matter? I don't need the money."

Laura came back around, bent her knees, and elegantly sat on her heels so she could look Sally in the eyes. "It's never about money. It's all about sharing information. Knowledge is worth a lot more than a paycheck. Come on board so you can find out how we tracked you down. We'll gladly trade with you in order to find out how you got so far into our system. Sure, money will change hands. But I'm not trying to buy you. I'm trying to entice you."

Her gaze was compelling. Sally could feel the charisma of this woman. She resisted it. "So entice me."

Laura stood back up and walked over to her window. She was silent for a moment, apparently absorbed in the view of the bay. Then she turned and faced Sally. "I have a project that requires someone of your caliber. But first, let me make it worth your while. Today, I will let you sit with the guy who got around your defenses. Tomorrow I'll tell you about my project. Give to get. And if you don't want to play, you can just leave. No hard feelings. Is that a deal?"

"Sure, lead on!"

Laura strode toward the door, past her surfer receptionist, and down the hall. Sally gave Ripley the command to heel and started for the door. The two of them lagged behind Laura as Sally tried to get through the thick carpet, but soon they caught up. Halfway toward the elevator Laura paused and key-carded a door. They entered a bullpen of cubicles, each containing a person intently typing on an ergonomic keyboard in front of a 22-inch flat-panel monitor. All you could hear was locust-horde clicking. Along one wall were five office doors. Laura walked down the aisle to the end office and knocked. Sally heard a click and the door opened.

They could see the occupant in profile, his attention completely focused on the screen in front of him. Dark, unruly hair, glasses, a white oxford shirt that needed some pressing, and an intense frown. "Just a sec, I gotta finish this one thing." The two women waited. And waited. Finally Laura said, "Edgar?"

He spun around. "Oh, Laura! I'm sorry. Gosh, I had no idea it was you. I'm so sorry—"

"That's all right, Edgar. I'm sure what you were working on is important. Is this a good time to talk?"

"Oh, sure!" He turned back and hit a couple of keys, and his screen went blank. "What is it?"

"I want you to meet Sally. I think she'd prefer it if I just used her first name. Sally, this is Edgar Allen."

Sally smiled and said, "Nice to meet you, Edgar."

"Sally is the person who penetrated into core level three yesterday. She and I are forging an alliance, so to speak. As part of that arrangement, I want you to show her how you diverted packets from her alarm detection system."

He continued to look flustered. "Are you sure? That's proprietary. I mean, I know it's your software. But I thought—"

"Show her, Edgar. Give her a copy of the program and the details about the hardware. Then see her out of the building. Sally, if you could come to my office tomorrow at ten, we can talk. Will that work for you?"

Again Sally nodded.

Laura turned and walked out of the office. Edgar kept watching her until she was gone. Then he turned to Sally. "Well, come around here, and I'll show you how it's done."

The next two hours were spent deep in conversation and demonstration about rotation, pointers, preamble generation, throughput comparison, and the adaptations necessary to modify a full-duplex, slotted, packet-switched WDM ring to convert RapidIO system addresses. Sally was in hog heaven.

But as Ripley and Sally were making their way back to her wheelchair-modified van, she was not thinking about system protocols. She was replaying the expression on Edgar's face as he watched Laura stride out of his office. It was a look of hunger.

CHAPTER TWELVE

Warren had had enough of whips, chains, and leather. He was getting carpal tunnel from flogging. Today he was taking a break from butt swatting and righting the wrongs of the world. He woke up to the bells playing across the street from his Berkeley apartment. He did his morning stretches and then started vacuuming and dusting the place. He knew that caffeine was coming as soon as he got his chores done. He was positively chirping when the telephone rang.

"Is this Warren Ritter?" It was a clipped man's voice.

"Speaking."

"You're the guy who does tarot card readings, right?"

He put on his headset, clipped the phone on his belt, and went back to dusting the built-in shelves in the corner of his bedroom.

"That would be me. I do consultations for seventy-five dollars an hour. Do you live in the Berkeley area?"

"Actually, I'm from out of town, but I saw your Web site, and I'm in town, and I'd like to see you. Do you have time?"

The caller wasn't freaked out by the prices on the Net. Warren could earn in a couple of hours what it might take half a day to make at his card table on Telegraph Avenue. Things were going along swimmingly. He glanced out his window as a Berkeley Farms delivery van slipped a gear climbing Euclid Avenue. He heard that same noise through his headset. Was this guy calling from nearby? Something was fishy.

Warren said, "Well, I think I might have some time this afternoon, but I will need to make a call and cancel some of my plans. Do you have a number where I can reach you? I'll get back in two minutes." He tried to sound eager, even though he had vampire bats in his stomach. Who had been pissed off? Was it the FBI?

"Sure." The caller gave a number Warren knew all too well. He used it often, since it was the only public phone booth in the area. Right down the street.

He disconnected and sweat spit out of his armpits. Who the hell was that person? Then he had him. The caller had used almost the same words on Phillip's answering machine. It was Troy, the punk who had chased him home from San Francisco and was trying to get Phillip's cards.

This punk might be on his way up here right now. Warren briefly contemplated going downstairs and kicking his ass. Once again he deeply regretted the reality that he wasn't a foot taller and a hundred pounds heavier. Sure, Warren thought, he's tough and wiry, but he was sure no bouncer. On the plus side, he had trained in martial arts. On the minus side, it was the wrong martial art: aikido. If Troy conveniently came running at him, Warren could flip him like crazy. But if Troy just stood there and pounded on him, he was in for a world of hurt.

That left Option B: He could run. Oops, make that "expedite a strategic retreat." That was something Warren excelled at!

As Warren started unlocking Phillip's safe he mused at the insanity of popular stereotypes. The conventional hero always has a lot of chest hair, and can't wait to walk up to total strangers and blast them away or bust them one in the kisser. From John Wayne to Stargate the only thing that changed was the weaponry.

What a crock! Real men knew when to retreat. It wasn't a sign of weakness. It was the sign of a devout commitment to victory, but only when they got to set the stage for it.

Warren opened the climate-controlled storage unit and stuck the bag that contained the cards in his pocket. He relocked the door. Let the guy try to break into that! Then Warren plucked a hair, wetted it down, and laid it across the top of the safe, so that one half rested on the door frame. Finally, he grabbed the backpack hanging by the door and exited, locking the dead bolt first.

No one in the hall, yet. He rejected the main staircase and went down the back stairs, all the way to the basement. He was totally in luck; no one was in the laundry room. Last year, he'd discovered a boarded-up hatchway that led from the laundry room into a deserted coal cellar. He closed the hatch behind him and pulled the battery-powered lighted makeup mirror from his escape pack and put it on a shelf. In under five minutes he was in a black wig, horn-rimmed glasses, a UC sweatshirt, and sporting an iPod.

He lifted up the slanted cellar door that opened to a narrow alley running along the back of the building. It was still unfastened from the last time he had used it. Then he clambered over the concrete wall into the little restaurant pavilion that included an open-air Thai restaurant, Chinese fast food, and Top Dog (simply the best hot dog on the planet). He stopped and grabbed a kielbasa to complete his disguise.

A gaggle of freshmen provided perfect cover. He walked in the middle of the giggling group as they migrated around the corner, across the street, and up to La Val's Pizza. From inside the herd he had the perfect view of the corner phone booth. No one was near it. He couldn't see Troy anywhere, not that he'd be able to ID him anyway. After all, he'd only glimpsed the blond crook from a passing car. Maybe Troy was already inside.

The rest of the morning was spent securing Phillip's cards. Warren took a bus to San Pablo and walked seven blocks north to Alfredo's Cycles. Alfredo took care of Warren's Aprilia RSV Mille motorcycle and a few other things. On the way he stopped in at a neighborhood grocery store and bought two rolls of black duct tape.

Al was used to seeing Warren in different-colored hair. It was far from the strangest thing the poor guy had to deal with. Al was "connected," and for his friends he was very trustworthy. Warren's bike was always gassed, oiled, tuned, and ready for a hard ride. And Warren's illicit belongings were always well secured. Warren contemplated leaving the cards there, but then he remembered the portable refrigerator unit. For some unknown reason Phillip had wanted them kept cool. Warren knew just the place for that.

He took off his wig and tossed it and the backpack into a locked cabinet he kept at the cycle shop. He borrowed a plastic bag from Al and put the red silk bag into it. He grabbed his leather jacket and helmet from the cabinet, locked it back up, and walked over to his bike.

Shiny ebony race bodywork with flame red lightning markings, gold rims and forks: It looked like it was going ninety just sitting there. Men are funny. When it comes to loving their kids, or their main squeeze, there's always something held back. Some tiny fear of being disappointed or let down that keeps them, even at best, only 99 percent present. But their toys; those men can love with abandon.

Warren stood there a moment, just admiring the sleek, fierce lines of his bike. He traced the way the backseat followed the line of the fat exhaust pipe, pointing to the heavens, and how the chrome shifter and pegs gleamed. His eyes traveled over the majestic sweep of the whole body, windshield, fairing, sexy rear taillight housing, and 138 horses straining at their leads. He thought, sheepishly, that he would never stare so adoringly for so long at Sally.

But this machine was good for a lot more than looks. If he was going to be Whipmaster, he couldn't imagine a finer set of wheels for the role. Beat the hell out of his Honda Civic. It might even impress Steele.

He wanted to crank it up and take off down Route 1 to Half Moon Bay and beyond, maybe all the way down to Big Sur. But he had promises to keep. Those damn cards took priority right now. So he headed into the warehouse district where Oakland bled into Berkeley.

Foster's Self-Storage had a bad reputation. You'd be more likely to find a frozen cadaver stored there than you would a piano. A big-mouthed, strung-out crack dealer on Telegraph had told Warren about the deals consummated in the alley in back of that two-story box. The speed freak also mentioned the regular police raids. It was a hangout for lowlifes, a drop point for dealers, and perfect for Warren's purposes.

He armed his bike's alarm system, chained it down, and walked into the dingy plywood cell that passed for an office. A gray

Formica counter divided the customers from the clerk. He was glad he had his jacket on now. The one quirky thing about Foster's was its massive air-conditioning unit. On the street they called it "Foster's Freeze." Rumor had it that it was installed to maintain the freshness of all the marijuana that the dealers stored there.

Gorilla shape, brown eyes, greasy black hair, and God knew what nationality, the clerk, Zog, got up from watching a rerun of *ER* and glared at him, saying nothing.

"I want a small walk-in on the second floor."

The cretin shoved a price sheet toward Warren. It had a large brown stain across the bottom of the page. Blood? The cheapest walk-in unit was listed at sixty-five dollars a month.

Warren laid two Franklins on the sticky counter. He invoked his crack dealer. "Zoë told me this would cover the first month's rent. I will be back next month with another two. But no paperwork."

Zog reached under the counter. Warren tensed. But the clerk brought up only a tagged key in his hand. Grabbing the bills and sticking them in his pocket, he slapped the key to unit 228 on the counter.

"Thanks."

The clerk said nothing, just lowered his bulk back down in his black vinyl Barcalounger and turned back to his TV.

Just down the hall from 228 was a wheeled dolly. Warren pulled it into the room and shut the door. Then he looked around at the ten-foot-tall, six-by-six cell. It was a plywood refrigerator, its air long dead. Above him a bare bulb stuck out of the wall over the door, enclosed by a thick wire mesh cage. Perfect.

From the inside pocket of his leather jacket he took the plastic bag containing the cards in the red silk bag. He wanted to look at the cards one more time before he hid them away. He took off his jacket and laid the deck on the floor.

He shivered, from more than the chill air. He leafed through the deck, pulling out the four cards he was looking for. One card had eight swords with their blades interlaced. Another portrayed a woman in a white cloak sitting on a throne, wearing a tiara. The third had a woman in a blue flowing robe holding up a star. Number four was his old friend: a man, hung upside down by his feet.

Warren touched the first one, the Eight of Swords, and closed his eyes. Out of the dark of his imagination swirled a scene: A girl lay on a bed, drugged, as gas fumes from below wafted into her bedroom.

He opened his eyes and both the vision and the smell dissipated. Damn, that was freaky! He closed his eyes and touched card number two, the High Priestess on her throne. Now he saw another bed, a hospital bed. A woman lay paralyzed on it, but she was much older, with a contorted face. This time the smell was antiseptic.

Warren quickly pulled his finger off that card and desperately looked around at the unfinished plywood on his storage room, to make sure the woman was just an illusion. He didn't want any part of that card!

He tentatively placed his finger on the third card, the Star. Now he smiled, as he watched a woman's hand caressing the tiny head of a little boy whom he knew very well: It was his grandson.

He arranged those four cards in a column. If he didn't close his eyes, they were just very old card stock, not windows into some parallel reality. Then he spread out the rest of the deck, facedown. Immediately, one card called him. It was visually exactly the same as the rest of the deck. But he knew it had something to tell him.

And he didn't want to hear it. He put that card on the top of the deck, still facedown. Then he put all the cards back in the bag, and wrapped them tightly in the plastic Safeway bag. He'd had enough divine guidance for a lifetime. He was taking a break!

He started winding the duct tape around the plastic bag containing the cards, first with the sticky side down, and then with the sticky side facing outward. He leaned the dolly against the wall and climbed up on it. Reaching up over the lightbulb, he slammed the sticky package onto the wall above the mesh cage.

He jumped down, opened the door, and wheeled the dolly out into the frigid hallway. As a last check he walked back into the room and looked around. Nothing but cold dust, unless you walked all the way in and looked back at the door. Even then, the black package stuck high on the wall wasn't very noticeable.

He left the storage facility and aimed his bike north. No cruising to Alaska for him today. This afternoon it was his turn to take care of his grandson, Justin. You gotta love a kid whose first word had been "giraffe" and whose second had been "Warren."

CHAPTER THIRTEEN

Sally's cell went off as she was pulling out of her parking space. She tapped the hands-free button. "Sally here."

"It's Vera. Can you come to the city? Thérèse wants to see you."

"I'm in the city."

"Um, ah, how are you dressed?"

"Like a young urban professional, why?"

"Oh, great! Thérèse's lawyer has agreed to smuggle you in as her paralegal. She has a business card all printed up and everything. Can you be at Jail Number Eight, 425 Seventh Street, in an hour? Her lawyer is Judy Hollister, and she'll be waiting out front for you."

"No problem."

It was called the Glamour-Slammer. Back in '94 it was the model of a detention facility, glass doors instead of bars, no long corridors, attractive architecture. But it still was a jail, no matter how pretty, housing four hundred men and women waiting to find out how long they were going to be in prison.

Judy met her out in front. They had no problem making it as far as the waiting room; this time nobody even challenged Ripley.

Then it was hurry-up-and-wait time. Judy pulled a file from her briefcase and began reading intently. Sally sat back and closed her eyes. Then she smelled dirt and rubber.

Flashbacks didn't happen often, not more than once a month or so. She heard the over-revving of the engine, the sound of tires spinning in the mud, then, after a flash of army green and black grease, the crack as the tires crashed down on her back. They'd been bivouacked for the night on the flat side of a small knoll. She was still in her bag when the clueless joyriding corporal had bounced his Humvee into the middle of their campsite, and put her in a chair for life.

She still broke out in a sweat whenever the memories flooded back. Rehab. A pea green hospital room, and a young Indian doctor shaking his head as he told her she would never walk again. The neutral expression of a nameless lying military bureaucrat who told her he was doing everything he could to bring charges on the driver. The sympathetic arrogance of those who still walked. And the faces of her roommates, broken, bitter, and trying not to cry.

Then she saw the wallpaper of her old apartment, slowly unpeeling from the top of the wall. The sound of splintering as she rammed her chair against the narrow doorways. Listening to the voices on her answering machine: the pity, the discomfort, and the excuses from those who once called themselves her friends. The phone growing more silent. Finally not even turning on the answering machine. She was only fit to live with other gimps.

Then she smiled. She remembered the day Thérèse burst back

into her life. It was about one in the afternoon. Sally was sitting at her computer debating whether to continue the self-study programming course or to start some serious drinking. Venge was rooting to stay at work: *Look, you're finally getting this stuff. In just a little while you're going to be able to royally destroy Corporal Walker's complacent little life. Don't quit on me now!*

Meanwhile Psyche, the wimp, just wanted relief from hopelessness that a tall glass of scotch could bring her. Psyche was winning when Sally heard a knock on her apartment door. She reached into a side pocket of her chair and wrapped her hand around the grip of her Beretta M9, the only memento she kept from the army.

Then she heard, "Hey, loser, why don't you answer your phone?"

Thérèse started banging at the locked door. Sally seriously considered staying quiet until she went away. Then Sally heard: "Look, baby cakes, you either open this door or I put a hole in it. And if you're not in there, then I'll just wait inside for you to come home. I win either way. Now roll your sorry ass over here and unlock this mother!"

Sally opened the door to a golden-eyed six-foot-tall redhead wearing moss green pants and a rusty orange silk blouse. Sally smiled and said, "You clean up pretty nice. Where are your leathers?"

Thérèse glared down on her. "Yeah, I try to look pretty when I'm visiting pathetic losers who are so wrapped up in self-pity they can't even answer messages from their best friend."

"Screw you!" Sally started to spin her chair around and wheel away. Thérèse grabbed onto one of the handles and stopped her.

"Not so fast. What's the matter? You're upset that I didn't do the 'Oh, you poor thing, blah, blah, blah!' routine? Yeah, yeah, you're paralyzed for life from the waist down. Big deal.

87

"Sally, you look like raw sewage. You're barricaded away in this moldy tomb. This place smells like piss and scotch. And you're sitting in one of the shoddiest chairs I think I've ever seen. Where did you get that piece of garbage, Goodwill?"

"The VA."

"Look, sister, I'm taking you to Berkeley, right after you get some respectable threads on. Today, you're going to get a decent set of wheels!"

"Counselor Hollister? You and your assistant can come in now."

They were escorted into a small pale blue room, furnished only with two chairs facing a Plexiglas window. Thérèse sat in a chair on the other side and a guard was stationed at the door behind her. The orange jumpsuit looked good on her, but she had dark circles around her eyes. She held her head high. They heard her voice through a speaker on the wall beside the window.

"Hi, Judy. I'm glad you made it. Brought your sidekick, I see." Then she smiled at Sally.

Judy said, "Thérèse, your arraignment is set for tomorrow morning. There we will enter a plea and the judge will set bail. Because of the crime and the nature of your profession, I'm sure the prosecution will make the case that you are dangerous and bail should be denied."

"What a pile of crap."

Judy wrote something on her pad. "Bail may be set at five hundred thousand or one million dollars. That means an up-front cost of fifty to a hundred grand. Some of it can be financed. Can you handle that?"

Thérèse frowned. Then Sally said, "Don't worry about the bail. That's already handled."

Thérèse started to say something, but Sally interrupted her. "Shut up, Ms. de Farge. Now is not a good time to talk." Thérèse closed her mouth.

Judy asked, "How are you doing?"

"I keep my own counsel, just like you told me to. The strong women in here leave each other alone. I don't care about the whiners. Besides, any one of them could cop a deal claiming that I confessed to them. "

Judy nodded. "Glad to hear it. You keep your cool and we might be able to get you out of here tomorrow."

Thérèse looked hard at Sally, then back at Judy. "How does my case look?"

Judy looked over at Sally. "I think my assistant has the latest report on that."

Sally said, "We've got three investigators on the case right now, and more can be called in if we need them. Once you get out of here I will bring you up to speed. Until then, just know that we are doing everything possible to find out who killed Mr. Hawkins."

Then Judy asked, "What happened that night?"

Thérèse shook her head. "Oh, it's really messed up. I did have a session booked with Greg. Then I got a text message that he was canceling. So I went down to Ocean Beach and took a long evening stroll. Then I went home, late, had dinner with Vera, and crashed. See, I'm really in deep trouble!"

Sally thought she detected the edge of a tear in one eye. She had never seen Thérèse cry. Thérèse abruptly stood up, turned around, and headed for the door.

Sally wheeled her chair away from the table and called out, "We're going to get you out of here, girl."

The guard stood up and stared at her. This was behavior unbecoming to an attorney.

Thérèse waved without turning around.

CHAPTER FOURTEEN

Sally called out, "Hold on, Heather, you've got to see this!"

The sun was a half hour away from dipping behind the Golden Gate Bridge. Sally was out training her dog at the Point Isabel Dog Park. She liked the shoreline and the constant distraction of romping, growling dogs all around her and Ripley. It forced Ripley to focus hard on her.

Heather came walking up in her usual outfit, torn blue jeans and tank top. She stopped when Sally said, "Stay right there!"

Sally leaned over and whispered, "*Zijdelings!*" to her dog. Then she started talking to Heather as Ripley sidled off.

"What I am trying to do is harness a natural instinct. Wolves in packs hunt in a particular fashion. The alpha male confronts the prey head-on, while the alpha female circles around to the back or side to attack. Now keep looking at me while Ripley gets into position. Don't look at her. And don't worry, I'll give her the jump up and lick command. She's almost in position."

Heather saw Ripley sneaking around, right up to the edge of her peripheral vision. When Sally yelled out, *"Vrij!"* Ripley covered the distance in two flying bounds and almost knocked Heather over as a hundred pounds of joyous muscle leaped up to lick her face.

CHAPTER FIFTEEN

Heather stood in front of the big concrete cube. You would have no idea who owned this monolith until you got close to the front door. There was a discreet brass plaque that read: CABOT SECURITY.

She seriously considered blowing the whole thing off. Then she heard Pink's voice in her head singing, "I don't want to be a stupid girl." Outcasts and girls with ambition. That was her! Hey, what could be the worst thing that happened? She strutted in, shaking free her hair and slapping on her ten-thousand-kilowatt smile. Look out, David Cabot, here comes the girl reporter.

She didn't get very far. The "reception" room was a small chrome cubicle mostly occupied by a bulky young man with a zit on the left side of his nose. He was sitting behind a shiny metal desk facing her.

"Welcome to Cabot Security. Do you have an appointment?" He looked as if he doubted it.

Heather knew she was wasting all her allure on this toady, but it was good practice for the big game to come. She tried to pretend that this guy really didn't have both a dermatological and an attitude problem. "Yes, thank you. I have an eleven o'clock interview with David Cabot."

He wasn't impressed. "Please empty your purse on the desk and open your briefcase."

What was she, a terrorist? She sighed. There was no way she was going to win this one except through submission. Good thing she wasn't carrying a stick of dynamite. She spilled out the meager contents of her handbag. He picked up her briefcase and examined it, looking for secret transmitters or something. Then he said, "Thank you. If you could just walk through this portal then you can retrieve your belongings."

That's when she noticed a slim door frame next to his desk. Airport security.

"Do I need to take off my heels?"

For the first time he smiled. She guessed he wasn't gay. She was making some sort of impact. "That's not necessary. This technology is far more advanced than that." He looked at his screen as she passed through. She wondered if he had it adjusted to see through her dress. Boys and their toys.

He must have hit some secret lever, because as she was stuffing everything into her bag a door slid open. She had made it past the first gate. But she was completely unprepared for what greeted her on the other side of those metal walls.

She walked into a lush open courtyard. The roof was retracted, and the only thing between her and the sky was a couple of stories of netting above her. Moss-covered rocks lined the gurgling stream in front of her. Birds surrounded her, cackling, cawing, and whistling. A flock of orange and yellow parrots flew up to the top of a eucalyptus tree. A flock! It was Disneyland's Jungle Cruise!

Zit Nose turned her over to the Incredible Hulk. Light on his feet and probably packing a small arsenal, he led her down a winding rain forest path past several intersections, turning and twisting through the labyrinth like a panther on the hunt. A very large panther.

They arrived at a door leading out of Adventure Land. Hulk opened it and Heather began climbing the staircase.

Living with Sally had rubbed off on her. "Not very wheelchair accessible, is it?" she asked her guide.

He had a deep, gravelly voice. "You're getting the blue-ribbon tour. There are more direct routes. It's just your lucky day, I guess."

Finally they got to a landing with just one door. Hulk opened it for her and she walked into a modern office, with one glass wall that overlooked the jungle.

Behind the desk sat David Cabot. As she later told Sally, "I don't know what I was expecting after that safari, Arnold Schwarzenegger or something. Not this roly-poly little bat-faced guy."

The girth of his waist was powerful testimony to years of dedicated Krispy Kreme grubbing. He was sporting a mullet hairdo, nasty short on top with greasy waves down the back. He was dressed in chinos and a light blue button-down oxford but was wearing fine Italian shoes.

Then he spoke, and she started to sweat. There was nothing lightweight about this man.

"Hello, Ms. Talbridge. So, you work at *Business West Coast Weekly*. Is Ted Weisberg still working there?"

Heather was glad she had checked out the *BWC* Web site last night.

"I'm sorry, I do freelance work for them. I'm not there full-time. But I have never heard that name before. Which department is he in?"

"How about Jane Diamond?"

"Sure, she just got the Tech Editor's job. A big step up for her, but she deserves it."

She must have passed some test.

"OK, I have seven minutes to give you until my next appointment. Fire away."

Heather thought to herself his next appointment was probably with Colonel Sanders. But she launched into the spiel she had prepared the night before to nudge the conversation over to the topic she really wanted to talk about.

"A piece on Greg Hawkins . . . beyond just an obituary . . . what's the impact on the industry now that he's gone?"

He sat right up. "This is off the record. If I see my name attached to this I will personally ram that Bic into your eyeball. Just call me a prominent cybersecurity executive. Right?"

Gulp! "Right."

His smile was far less than heartwarming. If vultures could smile they would look like that. "I'm so glad the SOB bought it. Hell, I'd have done it myself if I could have figured out how. He thought he was the Wal-Mart of security, pressuring us out of business, buying up the little guys, purposely underbidding to steal our clients. I was seriously considering legal action against him for that stunt he pulled with Intermediate Distributions Limited.

"And his damn wife is even worse. She's the bitch behind the throne, only it's all her throne now. Ask me, she probably did it. There's no throat she wouldn't slit on her way to the top.

"Now that you've got all that juicy background material, I'm ready to go back on the record. Say that David Cabot is very saddened by the passing of one of the great men in this industry, Greg Hawkins. He sends his condolences to Greg's widow and very able co-partner, Laura Hawkins. All of us who worked with him will miss him greatly, and I am sure Hawkins Computer Defense Systems will continue to do well under Mrs. Hawkins's skilled tutelage.

"And if that's all you need, we are finished. My next appointment begins in two minutes."

Heather thanked him sincerely, and told him that she would send him a copy of the article when it came out. All her instincts screamed that this guy was hiding something. So she did something that surprised her and seemed to startle him.

She said, "David, I would like to do an in-depth profile of you sometime. When could we schedule that?"

He looked at her without the angry glare. Then he cocked his head. Almost smiled. It might have been the first time he noticed that she was a cute young thing. He said, "I'd like that. Give me one of your cards. I'll be in touch with you."

Mr. Hulk walked her down through Amazonia and out to the street. Mission accomplished. Now she needed a shower.

CHAPTER SIXTEEN

Troy was good. Last night, when Warren had come back from babysitting, the apartment had looked almost untouched. Almost: He didn't know whether Troy had gotten the door to the safe open, but Warren's telltale hair left on the safe door was nowhere to be found. Troy had been there. Warren could feel his presence and the pressure of the air he had displaced. Threads of his energy had not yet dissipated. Either that, or Warren was hallucinating again. He was open to either interpretation.

Warren decided that this was not the right time for psychodiagnostics. He had to get ready for school. Today was the first session of Steele's new class at his Academy of Correction.

Warren had called Steele's number last night, and the professor himself (herself?) had answered. It asked no questions and did absolutely no qualifying exam. Warren guessed any friend of Vera's was OK by it. Or maybe his willingness to give Steele a credit card number was the qualifying exam. Anyway, Warren was in, and classes started at noon in the city.

No Boy Scout uniform today, just basic black. His leather jacket would be all the uniform he needed. He wheeled in front of the brick warehouse on an alley off Fifth Street. He armed his bike and then immobilized it with a Kryptonite chain-and-lock combo made of triple-heat-treated steel and wrapped twice around a convenient lamppost. If someone wanted this bike, he'd better be carrying an acetylene torch and expect to spend at least an hour getting through these bolt-cutter-resistant links.

Steele came out as he was tying his wheels down. Steele didn't say a word, but Warren could read the envy in those eyes. One point for the "he's-a-guy" camp.

"Get in here, you're late." Steele did a bang-up job of disguising jealousy, but Warren knew his bike had made an impression. "In here" was a large airy room with one brick wall and no windows but a roof that consisted mostly of skylight. A number of eyebolts were embedded in the brick. There was a staircase leading to an upstairs door, where, Vera had told him, Steele had its private apartment.

Warren was the seventh and final member of this group. No one looked like Torquemada. Three women, in jeans and T-shirts, ranging from anorexic to corpulent. Three guys, dressed in the same, ranging from nerd to stud. Igor was missing, as was the Marquis de Sade.

They sat on uncomfortable metal folding chairs facing the bricks. It walked in front of them. "I have a lot to teach you, and very little time to do it in. This class will meet four Tuesdays. In addition I will take each of you out one evening to watch you play in public settings. Pay attention to everything I tell you: People's lives, health, and well-being depend on it.

"I am going to do a scene. I want you to pay close attention.

Each of you must answer a question I will ask about the scene. If you cannot answer, I will hand you back your tuition and ask you to leave the class. There is no room in here for lazy inattention."

He called up to the second floor, "Elizabeth, come in now."

A woman in her thirties, a bit overweight but with clear blue eyes and long brown hair, opened the door, walked down the stairs and up to the brick wall.

"This is Elizabeth Camden. Take off your clothes."

She stripped down to her thong and bra. He then turned her toward the wall. Opening a wooden box, he took out rope and began tying her to the eyebolts in the wall. When she was secure, he took a flogger with knotted leather lashes. He began striking up her back, starting with her buttocks and ending with her neck. Then he stopped, turned around, and faced us.

"Each of you tell me something I have done wrong."

Immediately the thinnest woman said, "You haven't made this an emotionally safe play space for her at all!"

Steele turned back to Elizabeth and kissed her cheek. They could hear it whisper, "Elizabeth, I am so sorry. I know we rehearsed all this, but still it was awful. The only reason I put you through this is so that many people down the road won't be abused. But I so apologize."

She leaned her head against Steele's and said, "It was my choice."

"They'd better deserve you!" it growled.

Then Steele turned back to the group. "Correct. Next."

One of the men pointed out, "It looks like her right wrist is tied too tightly. Her hand is turning white."

"Exactly." Steele spun around and cut the rope around her wrist with a quick slash of its knife. Steele was good. The rope parted without leaving a scratch on her skin. Steele then untied her other binds. She stood there, rubbing her wrist. "If one of you hadn't noticed that in another minute I would have cut her down anyway. There is no excuse for restricting circulation. Tie the knots on yourself or with a fellow 'dom' until you learn the difference between handcuffing and injuring. Next."

A woman said, "You never checked in with her about how much stimulation she wanted."

At the same time, one of the men said, "You didn't set up safe words."

"Right and right. Who was I doing this scene for? My own arrogant ego, that's who. Get this straight, if you learn nothing else in this room: You top in order to serve your bottom. It is dangerous, hard, and sometimes exhausting work, both physically and emotionally. If you're in it for the kicks, at the expense of the precious person who has agreed to be your bottom, you should rot in the innermost circle of hell.

"Which is not to say some of the outer circles of hell aren't a lot of fun. There is no finer feeling in the world than taking your partner far beyond anything she or he ever thought they could endure. But it's a dance, a tango of pain and desire. You can't do it alone. Next."

The final woman said, "You didn't respect her confidentiality. You told us her last name."

"Very good." Steele smiled. "Our privacy is essential. It is a small world out there. Sometimes being outed as a member of our BDSM community can mean losing our jobs. Just ask any of the public school teachers who play with us. And, by the way, Camden is not her real last name. Next." He looked at Warren, but Studly, the other male student, spoke.

"You flogged her neck. Those cervical bones are close to the surface and should never be hit."

"That was the most dangerous part of this demonstration. I hated doing that. It violates my instincts. We did our best to protect her. Show them, Elizabeth."

She knotted her hair over her head, and then removed an almost transparent plastic collar from around her neck.

"Never strike joints, the face, the lower back near a kidney, the neck, the head, fingers, or toes. Striking those areas can be very dangerous to your bottom's life and health. At the very least poor aim might precipitously and negatively end the scene.

"And go easy on arms, on the very upper parts of the shoulders, on the legs, and on the upper part of the buttocks. These areas have fewer muscles and less tissue than the sweet spots: the middle and lower buttocks, the thighs, and the upper parts of the back."

Steele stood in front of Warren. "Well, have you anything to add to this discussion, or are you done with us?"

Vera had taught him well. He'd seen another three things that Steele had done wrong, but one of them was something Warren was betting no one besides Steele noticed.

"She has no way of releasing herself if something happened to you. If there was a fire or earthquake, or for some other reason you couldn't get to her, she would be trapped."

Steele turned to the rest of the class. "Warren brings up a particularly vulnerable topic that all tops must face. To discipline you need a healthy degree of arrogance, superiority, and pride. If you don't have it you will stink as a master or mistress. But that can easily lead to overconfidence. 'Nothing is going to happen to me! I am in charge. I am in control. If I am safe, then my partner is safe.' Bull!

"Don't act as though strokes, heart attacks, and natural disasters will never happen to you. We must always provide for the circumstance in which we would be incapable of rescuing our bottom. Often hanging a knife within reach is sufficient. I have yet to have one of my submissive partners draw it on me."

Steele then came up behind Warren's chair and placed a hand on his shoulder. "That was very good. Thank you, Warren. You win the prize. Come with me to a party tomorrow night. I want to see you in action. I'll meet you in front of the school at ten P.M."

It was an order, not an invitation. Several of Warren's classmates were glaring at the new teacher's pet. A highly competitive group here.

Steele went on, "Hubris, that is the human condition that we must come to terms with. Without it we are submissives. But it can end up causing someone's death. Perhaps that's what happened with the strangulation case that's all over the paper this morning. I know Thérèse de Farge, and a haughtier bitch you've never met. She might just have been inattentive and inadvertently killed her client. And that could happen to you. Far too easily."

Steele lifted its hand off Warren's shoulders and looked down on Warren. "You're a friend of Thérèse, aren't you, Warren?"

"No. I am a friend of Vera's."

A pat. Then the teacher went back to the front of the room. "Good. Now, the first step in creating a safe and secure play space is to design your alliance with your partner. I have four statements that I speak aloud to every partner before doing a scene with them. It's not just a speech. They have to agree with what I am telling them, not just acquiesce. Here's a hint: I remember them by thinking, 'Safe space, safe words, safe heart, safe body.' Here's what I say:

"One: You are under my protection. I will do all within my power to see that you are safe from permanent or severe harm or from intrusions from the outside world while we play.

"Two: I control the experience, but you always can slow it down or stop it by using your safe words. Of course you can also ask to intensify it. I may grant that wish, but I will always respect your need for limits.

"Three: You are precious to me, and I will see to it that you are held in my heart before we play, while we play, and after we play. I will give you emotional support even when you don't know how to ask for it, but please feel free to ask at any time.

"Four: This is a dangerous game we play. I will not go beyond my level of expertise in providing you delicious pain. But, should you be injured, I will see to it that you get immediate and excellent first aid and any necessary medical care.

"You would do well to make these statements your own."

Warren drove away from his first class confused. Steele was such a contradiction: superior and compassionate, vicious and gentle. At least he'd learned one thing. He could tell, every time Steele spoke her name, that it despised Thérèse de Farge.

4

THE NUMBER FOUR

THE UNIVERSAL energy that expresses itself in the number Four brings order and discrimination to the chaos of existence. Data is organized, tabulated, and analyzed until coherent patterns begin to emerge. We fear, in the darkest nights, that this whole creation is meaningless and random, and that our lives count for nothing. The logic of Four helps us regain a sense of the right order of things, and our correct seat at the table of life.

CHAPTER SEVENTEEN

I t was 10:00 A.M. exactly as Sally approached the perfect Aryan who guarded Queen Laura. This time he buzzed Sally right through with a smile and a nod to Ripley. Laura had laid a plastic runway down over her thick carpet, which made wheeling the chair much easier. That kind of consideration went a long way with Sally.

Laura was standing, facing out the window and speaking into an almost invisible wireless headset. "Tell Cabot to back off. If he doesn't, he'd better buy a fiddle because his empire is about to go down in flames. Now, no more calls till I am through in here."

Her voice switched from barbed wire to cabernet as she said, "Welcome, Sally. It's good to see you again. Was yesterday instructional?"

"Very. In about a week I should be able to harden my security system against any of your impressive tricks. Thank you."

"I'm glad." Laura walked over and wheeled her black mesh

swivel chair next to Sally's. She sat and then said, "I have been talking with some of your clients. A rather eccentric and anarchistic group of folks. But they all admire you very much."

"I'm surprised they would talk with you."

"Oh, we do intranet and Internet security for a number of progressive organizations and political candidates. It's all a matter of getting the proper introduction." They both smiled.

Sally waited silently. She was sure the pitch was on its way.

"Your reputation and their testimonials impressed me. Not to mention what you did coming into our system from the outside. How good are you at breaking down a defensive internal security system?"

Sally looked out the window and across the bay at the three-and-a-half-million-dollar view as she considered her answer. "No defensive system is impregnable, given enough time. The main problem is retaliation. I could break into FBI files, but not without getting ID'd and backtracked. And then, of course, I'd be sent off to Guantánamo.

"Assuming that you didn't have to protect your own privacy or your own hardware from counter-intrusive virus attacks, it's just a matter of patience to break through the defensive ice that protects the core administrative controller."

Laura nodded. "That's what I thought, too. As did every other hotshot programmer in this company. But none of us have been able to get into my husband's private files.

"As you can guess from the way that he died, Greg had many secrets. Many of them I don't want to know about. But, unfortunately, some of those files contain material about past, present, and future clients. I need that information, and I need it yesterday. So that's the little project I was talking about yesterday: breaking through my husband's security. I hope that's a challenge too delicious for you to pass up."

Laura was right. This sweetened the deal. Sure, Sally knew that she had to track down a murderer. But now there was icing on the cake. She was already thinking that if she could pull this off, it would give her access to the inner data of one of the world's biggest computer security companies. That spelled access to companies and organizations she'd never attempted to hack before.

"When do I start?"

"You're not going to be able to begin to penetrate this ice from an outside line. There are firewalls within our firewalls. So I'm going to let you use Greg's office and his entry into the system. We can go across the hall and start right now."

Sally's smile turned feral. "Lock and load."

The view from Greg's office was just a little more spectacular than the one from Laura's. Sally was thankful that the carpet wasn't quite as thick. She noticed that Laura had set out a bowl for Ripley. Next to it was a tall green bottle of Highland Spring Water from Scotland. This lady was getting into the bonus points territory!

Laura just opened the door and then left Sally alone. "Let me know if I can get you anything?"

Stock options? But that was just a snide internal remark from Venge.

Sally looked around. Well, she wasn't quite alone. Security cameras took in her every move. Although she noticed that they were positioned so that the camera couldn't see the keyboard on

Greg's desk. Smart move, he didn't want his passwords to be available to anyone.

Within minutes she was plunging into the virtual bowels of Hawkins Security.

CHAPTER EIGHTEEN

When are you going to stop playing Cops and Revolutionaries, Warren?"

He was sitting in the therapy room of his obnoxious therapist, Rose. It looked more like a living room than a clinical office, with comfortable couches and a window that looked across the water to Baghdad-by-the-Bay.

Rose was somewhere between his age and senility. Tonight she wore a chocolate silk dress with the body of a dragon graphically curling around it. She had him pinned with her steely blue stare and he knew she was waiting for a real answer from him, not one of his vain attempts at deflection.

He couldn't help himself. "When are you going to stop playing Hannibal Lector with me? I keep waiting for you to call me Clarice. What kind of mind game is that question?"

"Diverting, attacking, and answering me with a question. Nice job, Warren. Now stop playing with me and answer my question."

"I'm serious, Rose. Don't you think it's a weird question?"

Warren knew exactly where she was headed, but he'd be damned if he let on.

She knew he was dodging. "Still tap-dancing on the ceiling. OK, here is what I mean. Every member of the Weather Underground has turned himself or herself in, with the exception of one old geezer who probably died in a Mexican whorehouse. No one got jailed, except for Kathy Boudin and David Gilbert, who both ended up robbing banks with the Black Liberation Front. Bill Ayers is a Distinguished Professor at the University of Illinois. Mark Rudd teaches math in a community college. Bernadette Dohrn is a Professor of Law. Brian Flanagan owns a bar."

"Yeah, yeah, yeah, I saw the documentary, too. Do you know how many more people were in the Underground than ever get mentioned in all the media? Like me, for instance."

"My point exactly. You didn't kill two guards robbing a bank. No one has you on their most wanted list. You could change your name back to the name you were born with, Richard Green, call the FBI and confess, and then go around wearing 'Che Guevara Lives!' T-shirts and no one would give a damn. Why are you so continually secretive in a world where weathermen just give us the weather?"

"And what will you say when they haul me off?"

"That's the last question I want to hear from you tonight. Now focus. Why are you still in hiding?"

She wasn't going to let him slip out the back, Jack. He had to either make a big scene and stomp out or look at her question. He kind of preferred the stomping option. Only problem, she was like a rat terrier and he knew she'd come back to the subject in the next session.

"Well, we both know I'm a little crazy. But I think it's more than that. Living under the radar of police has been my modus operandi for over thirty years. I don't know who I'd be if I wasn't underground."

Rose nodded. "You have a daughter, a grandson, a sister, a serious love relationship, and some dear friends, not to mention a bullheaded therapist. None of that is compatible with the I'll-just-get-on-my-bike-and-ride-off-into-the-sunset mentality. Maybe it's time to set that old identity aside and find out who you really are."

Warren got up and walked over to the window, stalling for time, watching the lights come on in the city across the bay. Then he said, "You said something like that before. Something like 'life isn't safe, but I'm supposed to stick around, clean up my messes, and grow up.' I got the message."

"Turn around, Warren, and look at me. Good. That's *not* what I'm saying this time. You did stick it out, through some very rough times. I don't think you're going to run away anymore. But you're still identified with that rebel, that runner. Now you feel like you're a runner that's stuck in one place. What would it be like not to be a runner at all?"

"I don't know."

"How are you going to find out?"

Their session ended pretty soon after that. Warren left, not even able to remember what else had been said. He was just stuck with that question in his head: *"How are you going to find out?"* As he drove home, he thought of Phillip's cards, and especially the one that had called to him, the one he didn't want to look at.

Without really planning it, he drove to Foster's Self-Storage in Oakland. He went into his storage bin and shut the door. He pulled down the taped package and took out the deck. He felt like he was in some kind of altered state, a bit numb, a bit glazed, a bit scared. He turned over the top card, the one that had called him before.

A female angel floated in the heavens. Below her, almost as though it came out of her, was a bucolic country scene, cows, fields, and a tiny town in the distance. A tiny person was walking down the road toward the village.

He figured that this must be the World card, even though the image looked very different from the one he used. The one he was familiar with had a picture of an almost naked woman dancing in the heavens, surrounded by archetypal animal heads. Warren knew that the World card usually meant success, completion, and sometimes travel. But as he touched this card and closed his eyes, he got that weird semi-vision thing. Again the bleachy hospital smell, but now he saw Phillip lying in bed, still and lifeless. Then Phillip opened his eyes. Warren jerked away from the card.

He was angry as he tucked the card back in the deck and retaped the package to the wall. What the hell did that mean? And what did it have to do with his life?

Back home he got the answer to at least one of those questions. On his answering machine he heard a voice from the other side. "It ain't over till the fat priest reads extreme unction over your almost corpse. Oh, I forgot, the correct term has been changed from 'extreme unction.' Now it has been watered down to something like 'anointing of the sick.' God forbid that anyone might imply that the poor soul might actually be dying." It was Phillip.

"Anyway, you may have guessed by now that I have not shuffled off this mortal coil. The doctors flocked around me like vultures around fresh roadkill. While I lay etherized upon a table, they re-plumbed my heart, which had stopped because of a life of excess. And while they were at it, they removed that pesky brain tumor, since I clearly hadn't much to lose at that point. All in all a wonderful time was had by everyone.

"Were you successful at rescuing my cards before one of the parasites snagged them? There are five or six gentlemen on this planet who ruthlessly pursue them. I hope you didn't run afoul of any of them.

"I should like to see you sometime soon, perhaps in a few days. The tubes in my chest make me less than pleasant company right now, except when the morphine gives me some breathing room. As the drug is starting to wear off now, I will bid you adieu." Click. Silence.

He lived.

CHAPTER NINETEEN

A gentle hand touched Sally's shoulder and she jumped. She looked up to see Laura holding a glass of deep red wine out to her with the other hand.

"You have been in here for too many hours. It's time you stopped for tonight."

Sally took a sip. "Oh my God! What kind of wine is this?"

Laura smiled a Mona Lisa smile. "I know. Isn't it enchanting! A gold medal winner. It's a 2004 Trinchero, Mario's Reserve Meritage, a Bordeaux-like cabernet blend. Just wait a decade and it will be breathtaking. One of my indulgences."

Sally took another sip, and then just breathed in the heady fumes. "It's pretty breathtaking right now. Thanks."

"How's it going?"

Sally sighed. "Not well. Did you know his password is randomly generated and changes every five minutes? I can't figure out how he knows what it is. So far I can't find a back door into the part of this system that protected and encrypted his files. Once I get to the files I can break the encryption; that's just a matter of computing muscle and time. But I haven't made a dent in the ice wall."

"Welcome to the club. Why don't we just call it a day. Come on into my office, and I'll have a little snack sent up. You've earned it."

The "snack" was roast lobster in a tarragon sauce with trumpet mushrooms and soybeans. Sally wondered if Laura would mind if she offered Ripley a tidbit. Probably not a good idea. So she waited until Laura's back was turned before she slipped Ripley a bite.

Laura opened her office refrigerator and poured a 2005 Viansa chardonnay, Estate Carneros. Sally liked wine, and loved food, but this was way out of her class!

"Is this from the company cafeteria?"

Laura laughed. "No, Gary Danko sent it up. I was counting on you to join me. I want us to get to know each other a little better."

On a pleasantly mellow drive home, Sally reflected that "getting to know each other" had ended up more like a monologue on her part. She was making a rotten detective. She'd learned very little. But right now she didn't care. It had been too long since she had enjoyed an evening with a woman quite that much. Venge kept saying, *Now* that's *a woman who knows how to live!* Sally could still taste the crème brûlée.

The ring of her cell phone disturbed her savoring. She pushed the button for her speakerphone.

"Yes?"

"Hi, baby. It's good to hear your voice. God, so much has happened to me today. I've got a lot to tell you. Can we get together tonight and talk? Oh, and how was your day in the city?"

Listening to Warren in a needy place was the last thing she

wanted to do. "I'm sorry, Warren. Actually, I'm kind of bushed. Tonight really wouldn't be such a good time."

"Oh, OK. Sure. Well, are you OK?"

"I'm good. I got access to their computers. Maybe in a couple of days we will find out the inner secrets of Mr. Greg Hawkins."

"Good for you. Nice job. Well, hopefully we can get together tomorrow night—oh no, I forgot, I have to play 'Steele's Pet Attraction' at some party tomorrow. Anyway, I'd love to get together sometime soon to talk."

"Me, too. Just not tonight. Call me tomorrow."

"Will do. Have a restful evening."

"I will, thanks. Good night, Warren."

A slide show of emotions flared up: remorse—she was not being totally honest with Warren; guilt at blowing him off when he needed her; resentment—why did he call right now, and interrupt her nice evening? It wasn't fair. He spent the day fooling around with Thérèse's little pixie while she spent the day at a keyboard. After a while she just stopped thinking about Warren. It was more pleasant to remember that lobster. As she drove up to her house, she noticed the paint was looking a little shabby.

CHAPTER TWENTY

The jungle inside Cabot Security was tame compared with the concrete jungle outside those walls, Heather thought to herself. She was exhausted. Her feet hurt. The two interviews she had done today were a bust. And she was convinced that someone needed to dump massive amounts of saltpeter into the reservoirs that serviced San Francisco. She had been continually hit upon by geeks, creeps, and taxi drivers.

Through some miracle the BART car she was in was populated with tired women, none of them actively lesbian. She couldn't take one more pickup line. Even thinking about it brought some of the worst ones to mind. A parade of images came back to her:

First there was pink-cheeked Mr. Enthusiastic, looking younger than her, she thought he was probably in his early twenties. His razor probably lasted for years. He came bouncing up to her and blurted, "So there you are! I've been looking all over for *you,* the woman of my dreams!" *Gag me!*

Mr. Sincere, approaching her while she was drinking her Starbucks. Decked out all tweedy. "Excuse me, I don't want you to think I'm ridiculous or anything, but you are the most beautiful woman I have ever seen. I just felt like I had to tell you." Why did she have the feeling that she was the sixteenth girl he'd tried that old line with today?

Her favorite, and it almost worked, was the messenger boy on his bike who pulled over as she was walking along and shouted out, "Hey, good-looking. Do you believe in love at first sight, or should I shoot around the block and drive by again?"

Heather smiled at that memory. Then she opened her briefcase and started to write her notes into her laptop.

```
To: Sally and Warren
From: Heather
Subject: Report on Wednesday Interviews


Here's the bottom line on two of our possibili-
ties.
    Walter Petoskey runs Computer Defense America.
Yes, a tried-and-true, good-old-boy Republican
operating right in the heart of San Francisco/
Gomorrah. Old for a techie, looked in his forties.
Suit, tie (even in this heat), button-down collar
on a shirt with too much starch. A face that's
easy to forget.
    OK, Sally and Warren, I know you guys' politics,
and I know you'd both love to pin it on him. Un-
fortunately, according to Walt, he loved Greg
Hawkins like a brother. They were negotiating some
```

defense contract together. I gather Greg was spear-heading the negotiations. Greg's death hit him where it really hurts, the wallet. He says the deal is dead. A deep and abiding grief here for lost profits. And no, I was not interested in a little drink after work, thank you very much. Anyone who calls me "Missy" should join Greg in the noose.

Spencer Woodard is CEO of Data Security Transnational. Young, prematurely balding redhead. Probably has plenty of chest hair. Works out, or takes steroids. Dorky-looking, in a hunk-wannabe kind of way.

Got very red in cheeks when I steered the conversation around to Greg Hawkins. Stopped talking for a while and then went off-the-record. (Yeah, right!) Hawkins has been trying to buy him out. Why is this guy telling me this? Is he suicidal, yakking to a reporter? And when is he going to stop looking at my breasts? He goes into the Woodard-as-hero story about how he fought off the hostile takeover. Judging from the shabbiness of the chair I had to sit in, that battle cost him more than he was willing to admit. So he's still on the island. Oops, I forgot, Warren; you don't have a TV, so *Survivor* metaphors probably go zooming past. Any-way, he's still in contention as a candidate. Gotta say, he's a wimp, though. And after he asked me, "So, what are the chances that we can engage in anything more than just conversation?" his attrac-tion factor sank into negative numbers.

She closed her laptop and shut her briefcase. Only halfway through the tunnel. She leaned back and closed her eyes. She was relieved that she had to take tomorrow off from sleuthing. She had a trig final at school. That should be a lot more relaxing! Then, Friday, she had a couple more faux interviews scheduled. Then this weekend she was on Justin babysitting duty. She hoped Sally or Warren would catch the bad guys and that she could get out of this gig. Adulthood sucked.

5

THE NUMBER FIVE

FIVE IS a powerful number in magical traditions. One of its names in the kabbalah is Fear. You use a pentagram to call up demons to serve you. The five-sided Sigil of Baphomet is the symbol of the Church of Satan. It is strength that is relentless, harsh, and unyielding. There is no compassion, no gentleness, in the unfolding of this principle of karmic law. Mere humans despair in its inhumane presence.

CHAPTER TWENTY-ONE

Phillip looked worse than the last time Warren had seen him, and he looked dead then. His head was bandaged, as was his chest. He was pasty and almost gray. But his eyes were open.

His voice was weak. "Hello, Warren. Surprised?"

Warren smiled. "Phillip, I'm glad you're still with us."

"And my cards?"

"Safe as safe can be, in spite of the attempts of a man named Troy who seemed to think they rightfully belonged to him."

"The worst of the pack of hyenas. Always nipping my heels, always trying to get their claws on my deck."

"How come they haven't succeeded before now?"

Phillip turned away and looked out the window for a moment. "How do I put this? It's not like I own the deck. It's more like the deck chose me. As long as I am alive, other people's plans and plots to steal the deck always seem to go awry. I don't know what would happen if I died, but I bet the pack would choose someone else."

"I had no problem getting it."

"Yes, and that may not be a blessing. If the pack chooses you, life is not always very pleasant. As you may have already found out."

"Those cards are scary! Look, do you feel good enough to answer a question?"

"I tire pretty easily, but I am completely bored. So I will do my best. Which card has attached itself to you now?"

"A couple. One, the Hanged Man, I know about. But what does it mean to get the World card from this deck?"

"Ah, Sophia. The closest that the Judeo-Christian culture ever came to worshiping the goddess Kali. And a vile heresy in the eyes of the Catholic Church. The church considered the Gnostic gospels heretical doctrines, and believing in them was one of the greatest of all sins.

"Understandably so. You see, according to Gnostic belief, this God that the Catholic Church finally came to espouse was a false god. An American poet, Phyllis McGinley, described him perfectly: 'Not God the Father or the Son but God the Holy Terror.'

"As I interpret the Gnostic view of creation, the Big Bang was the moment when Sophia forgot that she was a part of the unfolding presence of the true God. She was lost, and in her shock and pain she created substance and spirit. Out of these, manifestations naturally evolved on an even crasser, more materialistic level. The ancients called these manifestations Earth, Air, Fire, and Water. We call them Matter, Space, Energy, and Time.

"Her most unfortunate creation, however, was her offspring. The God of punishment, hellfire, and retribution was the false and evil son of Sophia. Gnostics called it Ialdabaoth, the Demiurge. He had a lion's head and a serpent's tail. Today it is he who rules, not Sophia, and not the divine presence. He's forgotten his parentage and imagines that he is the supreme one. His arrogance, pride, and incompetence have resulted in the sorry state of the world as we know it, and in the blind and ignorant condition of most of mankind.

"Sophia, seeing the horror she unleashed, came back to this place she had created and reached into the heart of her son, into the heart of the Demiurge, trying to rekindle the knowledge of his connection with Universal Love. She failed and was trapped down here. In that aspect of her, she is called the Wandering One.

"The Christ, as the manifestation of the Universal Principle of Love, was brought into this veil of tears to open our eyes to our true nature. His goal was to bring all of Sophia's creation back into universal consciousness. Go to most white, fundamentalist Christian churches on Sunday and you'll see how well that mission is going. They give lip service to the guy up there on the cross, but it's that Old Testament God of sin and eternal damnation, of intolerance and retribution, that they revere and seek to emulate.

"This lecturing is tiring me. It's your turn. Tell me about how she showed up in your life."

So Warren filled him in. Phillip's eyes almost closed, but Warren knew he was harnessing his energy to take in every word. Then came a long pause.

With his eyes still closed, Phillip said, "There are only two cards in the deck whose meaning stays the same regardless of whether they appear reversed or upright. One is the Sun, the manifestation of our personal soul's journey through life. For our ego, nothing is ultimately ill, because everything has a lesson in it we need to learn. The other is the World, manifestation of the Soul of Creation. When Sophia shows up, the Mother of All Living Things, the Womb of Creation, the Revealer of Perfection, then the true nature of your self is about to be brought to light. Look out, it won't be what you expect."

Phillip opened his eyes as though that was an effort and smiled at Warren. "I am exhausted now. But thanks for the excellent inquiry. And take care of my cards for a little while longer, if you would."

"Of course, Phillip. As long as you need me to."

CHAPTER TWENTY-TWO

Sally pushed her chair away from the desk. Her second day at cracking this computer system was not going well. She rubbed her eyes with the tips of her fingers, and then looked out the late Greg Hawkins's floor-to-ceiling window. The city, scrubbed and sparkling, beckoned to her.

She scratched Ripley's ears and then asked her dog, "If I hit the glass hard enough, do you think I could just crash through and fall to my death?" The prospect seemed particularly appealing right now. Ripley wagged her tail, agreeing with the idea.

Sally had finally met her match. Greg Hawkins had her checkmated at every turn. His files had an internal intrusion detection system. Every attempt to find the path to his files turned back on itself, and left her where she started. It was defense in depth, utilizing a devious cascading principle, which meant that every time she got through one barrier she had to start from scratch with the next one.

She couldn't get into critical parts of the registry; entry to the files wasn't on the access control lists; she couldn't use her usual tricks to work her way around the wall in AIXv3. Hell, it took her this long just to find the crypt in which most of the files were stored. Every one of his files that she did find was encrypted in the military-grade AES-256 format. She could break that, but the bulk of the material was behind a vault door she could not hack.

There were none of the typical software vulnerabilities, no buffer overflows, no format string vulnerabilities, no integer overflow, no code/command injection. It was elegantly written code, the sweetest she had ever seen.

This security was beyond A-1 status. She remembered one of the lessons she'd learned in the classes she took in computer security. One of her teachers had said, "The only truly secure system is one that is powered off, cast in a block of concrete, and sealed in a lead-lined room with armed guards—and even then I have my doubts." But he'd never seen this one.

She was afraid that this security system might be based on an ancient (fifteen years old or more) operating system's kernel technology. If that was the case, it might just be impenetrable. The security would be built into the hardware itself and therefore inaccessible.

As the afternoon sunlight streamed in on her, she dropped her head into her hands. Heather was taking a test, Warren was out flailing someone, and she was sitting, immobile and powerless, just taking up space in a dead man's office. Meanwhile police were gathering evidence, prosecutors were building a rock-solid case, and Thérèse was on a one-way trip to a lethal injection.

CHAPTER TWENTY-THREE

Jump on, let's ride."

Warren had called Steele earlier and had an incomprehensible conversation with it. Something like, "Dress code is fetish, rubber, leather, vinyl, cyber, gothic, fetish drag, high formal (top hat and tails), historical fetish, role-play, and cosplay. No blue jeans. Pick me up in front of the school at eight. I've got my own helmet." Yes, sir, ma'am. At least Warren understood the date and place.

Vera had outfitted him: his Verdramini motorcycle boots, a full-length leather duster, NATO-style black combat trousers, and a gray fitted sleeveless tank top with a discreet logo that read: WHAT'S YOUR EDGE?

Steele was standing outside the school when Warren wheeled up. It jumped on the back of the bike and said, "Head for Marin." Steele leaned hard into the turns and they booked.

Warren drove like a fiend with one quarter of his brain while reviewing Vera's instructions with the other three quarters. They'd had an intensive prep session that afternoon to prepare him for his "coming out" party. He could see her pixie face as he remembered her words.

"This sounds like a semi-private party, so rules may or may not be posted, but you need to know proper etiquette, regardless. No touching anyone without their prior permission. No touching anyone else's toys without their permission. No talking about anyone else's scene, even as a quiet aside. No getting in anyone's space, especially after a scene when they are doing aftercare. Keep everything clean and for God's sake, no gawking! Your cover will be busted in a second if you act like a rube!"

They flew across the bridge and out Sir Francis Drake Boulevard. Soon they were in the hills, with all the million-dollar bungalows behind them and farmland ahead. After a couple of lefts and rights into smaller and smaller lanes, Steele pointed to a farmhouse set back off the road. The windows of the white house were glowing welcome and the driveway had those amber lights along it to guide those with severe night blindness. Warren's stomach tightened one more notch.

Parked behind the house were a flock of BMWs, Volvos, and Mercedes. This was clearly not a grunge crowd. A rotund gentleman opened the back door as they peeled off their helmets and locked them on the bike. As Tartuffe welcomed his companion, Warren opened one of the bike's rear compartments and took out the small black medical bag that Vera and he had prepared.

"Ah, Steele. It is a delight to see you again. And you bring a protégé, I assume."

Steele just nodded. Warren was left to introduce himself, using only his first name, as Vera had coached him to do. They walked into the country kitchen, past the walk-in refrigerator, the granite countertops, and a restaurant-sized Viking stove.

The fat man said, "I'm Lawrence. Welcome. Your timing is excellent. We've just about finished the superficial chitchat and we're starting to get down to business. Steele, are you going to show Warren around?"

"No."

"Your usual loquacious self, I see. I'll have Adia give you the tour. *Adia!*"

A tall, slightly overweight, fortyish redhead glided in, sporting matching coral lipstick and fingernail and toenail polish, and dressed in a tight white vinyl dress with severe lacing around the waist. "Yes, Lawrence."

"Show Warren around the place. You are free to play with him if you so desire, assuming he wants to play with you."

How nice. He was being handed a slave. Warren wasn't sure what the correct response to this was. To whom did he say thank you? So he just nodded and tried to look cool, knowledgeable, and savage.

Adia turned to him, looked at him, and perhaps through him. Then she dropped her gaze.

"If you wish I will show you the play rooms."

"Lead on."

Warren knew what "play" meant, and it didn't involve charades or Twister. But he was totally unprepared for the living room. It was normal. Nice beige leather overstuffed chairs and sofa. Embers of a fire galling and gashing away in the brick fireplace. And a crowd of normal Marinites, drinks in hand, standing around socializing. Was this a joke?

As he looked closer he saw that the dress was not exactly normal.

Some of the men were decked out in smoking jackets and looked like Regency vampires. Others were in well-pressed Desert Storm camouflage. The rest of the crew were in basic black leather. The dresses on the women were either slit up the side to around the armpits or extremely short. He discovered another difference when Adia handed him a drink: carbonated orange mango juice. No alcohol tonight.

A gentle pull on his arm and they were headed for the spacious stairway going downward.

"Wait."

Warren stopped them at the head of the stairs. There, hanging just to the left of the entrance, was a small framed lithograph. Warren paused to examine and read it. Either it was an excellent facsimile or it was the product of some unscrupulous art dealer. It was a page from an early edition of William Blake's *Songs of Experience.*

Warren had heard of book cannibals who bought rare manuscripts and then hacked them to bite-sized pieces, so any upper-middle-class bozo could own a shred of an original. Like cutting the Mona Lisa into one-inch parcels.

However onerous Warren thought this practice might be, he couldn't help admiring the sense of irony that resided in the owner of this slice of Blake's genius. In the picture, steer and sheep drank thirstily at the top of the page and frogs cavorted in a stream on the bottom. A vine twisted up one side connecting the two images. In between, in Blake's precise slanted script, were these words, oddly appropriate for where the two of them were headed:

THE CLOD AND THE PEBBLE
Love seeketh not Itself to please,
Nor for itself hath any care,

But for another gives its ease,
And builds a Heaven in Hell's despair.

So sang a little Clod of Clay
Trodden with the cattle's feet;
But a Pebble of the brook,
Warbled out these metres meet:

"Love seeketh only Self to please,
To bind another to its delight,
Joys in another's loss of ease,
And builds a Hell in Heaven's despite."

The basement was massive and finished in concrete block. How urban. Along one wall were five small rooms, all with doors that had large windows inset into them. The side rooms opened onto a center court. There were couches and chairs scattered around the court, interspersed with whipping posts, crosses mounted on the wall, a set of stocks, three heavily padded prayer benches, a cage just large enough for one person to stand in, and several massage tables with eye hooks for attaching restraints. Warren acted like he saw this stuff in most basements that he visited. Next to the washer and dryer, right?

"Nice layout."

"Come see the breakout rooms."

Each room had a different theme. The first one was the Medical Office: antiseptically white walls, white soundproofing tile with inset neon lighting, shiny linoleum white tile floor, examining table, eye chart, white metal drawers marked: BANDAGES, FIRST-AID SUPPLIES, SCALPELS. Free-standing high-intensity lights, blood pressure cuffs, a walker, and a box with electrodes hanging down from it on a rolling stand.

Portal number two opened up to a huge shower room, tiled on the floor, walls, and ceiling in light blue tile, except for the large drain in the center of the room. A number of hoses and shower fixtures adorned one wall.

The third room was the Gym, complete with several pieces of Nautilus equipment and two weight benches with eyebolts welded on them to accommodate restraints.

The Dressing Room was next: a long mirror and makeup shelf along one wall, a double-wide full-length mirror on the other wall, frilly chairs, a thick pink carpet, and a closet filled with dresses, suits, and shoes. The only disconcerting items in this scene were the pink leather prayer bench and a hat rack with whips and floggers hanging next to the feather boa.

Finally, the Bedroom. Damask brocade covered the wall. Electric candelabras lit the room. One wall was mirror except for the cage in the corner. Another mirror looked down from the ceiling. The king-sized bed had a number of handcuffs and ankle cuffs hanging from the sturdy cast-iron head- and footboards.

"Very nice."

"If you would like, there is a quiet place by the fire where we could talk."

She was feeling him out to see if he would be a good play partner, or a jerk. "Sounds good. Let's go."

One corner of the central room had a wine red Vermont Castings wood stove merrily warming the love seat placed in front of it. They settled in. Since he was the dominant, Warren figured he better take the lead. After taking a sip of his soda he said, "Adia, since we really didn't get introduced, tell me something about yourself."

"I'm a dental hygienist." They both laughed. "I know that should make me a top, but torturing people is what I do for a living. Inflicting pain gets boring after a while. I'm Lawrence's weekend slave. I come to events like this to relax and let myself be ruled by someone else for a change."

She didn't ask, like a good submissive, but Warren sensed she wanted to find out a bit of his story. "I'm a tarot card reader in Berkeley." He could see her eyes brighten in interest. That must be more provocative than "I'm an accountant in San Francisco."

"I've also been a truck driver and a long-line fisherman for sablefish and halibut off the coast of Alaska. I played the stock market until I was rich enough to stop."

Enough with the small talk. He'd established his testosterone-laden credentials. He said, "I would like to play with you, Adia, but in a rather different way. Let's see if this is something you might want to do. It involves a lot of mind play. I'll use sensory deprivation and bondage, but no gagging. You will be undressed and I will use mild pain. I will touch your body everywhere, but not penetrate with any object. What else do you need to know to make this safe for you?"

He had passed some kind of test. She looked intrigued. "Interesting. Yes, OK. I'd like to play. Here are my limits. My safe word is 'red.' Nothing original there. 'Yellow' means 'slow down, I may be getting overwhelmed.' 'Green' means 'if you want to do more, you can.' I'm not on any medication, and I have no health issues. I am HIV negative. I already took my contact lenses out. Please, no cutting, burning, marks, scars, knife, hot wax, or fire play. I don't know you that well, yet. I don't like age play, but other role play is fine. Will this involve sexual activity?"

Warren was very glad she didn't like age play, since he didn't have the slightest idea what that was. He hoped he wouldn't do it accidentally. This scene sure as hell wasn't going to involve sex. He doubted that he could perform in this circus.

He answered, firmly, "There will be no exchanges of fluids, other than perhaps a kiss. I also am HIV negative, but that won't be an issue in this session. I expect it to last for about an hour. I will hang a knife near your left hand, in case you need it in an emergency. Otherwise I will be very displeased if you touch it, even accidentally. Do you understand?"

"Yes."

"From now on address me using my name: 'Yes, Warren.'"

"Yes, Warren."

"Is there anything else you need to know or say before we begin, Adia?"

She thought for a moment. "Is this a public or private scene, Warren?"

"Very public."

She smiled. "Good, Warren. I like those." Just the girl he needed for this little exercise.

Warren and Vera had spent a long afternoon planning this scene. Truth to tell, Warren really didn't enjoy flogging away on women's butts. But he didn't want to let out his preference for vanilla sex over chocolate. So the two of them came up with a scene that would captivate Steele without exposing Warren's lack of motivation.

He took Adia by the hand and they walked over to one of the crosses mounted on the wall. He opened his bag and hung the dagger on an eyebolt over the left arm of the cross. Then he took out the fur-lined blindfold and tied it on Adia.

He took out two lengths of soft cotton rope and tied her arms to the cross braces, making sure that the rope was not too tight. She had room to move her wrists slightly. Then he said, "Adia, I am now going to place the handle of the dagger in your hand. This will be the last time you touch it until the end of the scene, unless I give you permission. Nod if you understand?"

She nodded. The handle was easily within her reach. Now came the interesting part. He put earbuds in her ears and then tied on earmuffs. He took out a stopwatch and an iPod and set them on a coffee table near his station. He took out his cheat sheet. He plugged in the headphone cord and then started both the timer and the iPod. Then he watched Adia. Ten seconds later, right on schedule, she nodded.

He looked down on his sheet. On the top of the first page he read:

00:10 She nods.
00:17 Run fingers through her hair.
00:21 Stroke her left cheek.
00:30–1:45 Take off her dress. Don't hurry, you've got all the time you need.
1:45 Stroke her right breast, and then lightly pinch nipple.
Wait until she nods and then pinch left nipple.

All he had to do was watch the clock and follow instructions. Soon others in the common room came wandering over to watch. Steele was watching from the stairs. One bystander was impolite enough to ask, "What's she hearing?"

Warren glared at him and he was properly abashed. Bad manners to interfere with a scene in any way. The beauty of this technique was that it provoked the imagination, both in the slave and in those watching. The watchers had no idea what she was hearing. That, in its way, was quite compelling. After a while Warren had a group pulling up chairs to watch the show and to create scenarios in their own minds for what was going on. Adia's face got flushed and she began to pant. Perfect.

Thérèse specialized in using this form of mind play, and had collected a rich library of digital sound effects. Vera had mixed it and downloaded the hour-long mix into his iPod. They had rehearsed this and refined the time line.

What was going on in Adia's inner world was perfectly attuned to an exhibitionist, which many submissives are. Adia was told that Warren was wearing an intercom and she was wearing the earbuds so he could communicate with her while she was in earmuffs. In her world, it sounded to her like Warren was calling people over until a large crowd gathered. They were all admiring her, as he displayed her body.

He would comment on how she was getting aroused and there would be a swell of admiring noises from the crowd. Suggestions were thrown out from the bystanders, and he would reject some and try others out. Soon she heard the sounds of couples in the crowd getting excited just watching her, and sounds of their lovemaking joined the mix. A huge orgy was erupting, all focused on Adia and her body, as he aroused her, tantalized her, and stimulated her with caresses and with pain. After a while the commotion died down, and she could hear some people wandering off.

Finally the hour was over. Warren took down the dagger. He took off the nipple clips, removed her earmuffs, took out the earbuds, and packed them all away in the bag with the iPod. Then he took off her blindfold and she saw a number of people still sitting around, watching her, adding a nice touch of reality to the fantasy she had been listening to.

She looked around in wonderment, and then looked at Warren.

"Warren, I can't believe that just happened."

He untied her and put his arm around her, saying, "Come on, let's go over by the fireplace and just be together." They sat, and she curled into him. "That was so amazing. I never . . . Oh, Warren, thank you so much."

He stroked her head and she began to cry gently as she cuddled more tightly. They sat like that for about a half hour. It was very sweet and tender. This was such a strange world.

On the ride home Steele was silent. As Warren dropped it off in front of the school, all it said was, "Good job, Warren." High praise indeed from the stingy SOB.

Going back over the bridge to Berkeley, Warren started to drop. He felt sad, and heavy. It didn't feel like one of his regular depressions. This was one with a very fast onset: He went from feisty to crappy in seven seconds. He felt used up, low, and exhausted. He decided on a two-step program. Step number one: Don't follow up on that seemingly excellent idea to drive off the bridge into the bay. Just get home and get to bed. Step two: Tomorrow, find out from Vera if this was normal or if he needed to adjust some meds.

CHAPTER TWENTY-FOUR

Sally was alone. Everyone else had left the office. A security guard had just knocked on Greg's office door to check in on her. He would be back on this floor in eighty minutes, plenty long enough for her.

She looked up at the security camera and then at her computer screen. There were the folks in security, watching *their* screens. For the next forty-five minutes the screen for this office would be playing a loop of her working away, studiously. The rest of the screens would be featuring last Wednesday's camera feed. In other words, empty hallways. They should never have given her total access to the system. Jury-rigging this escapade had taken up a lot of her second afternoon's work.

She wheeled down the hall, Ripley trotting after her. Edgar's digs first. She had done a deep background search on him. At his desk she pulled out her list of possible log-in codes. People inevitably figured they were so clever that they didn't need no stinking random number codes. Edgar was no exception. Fifteenth try and she had it: the mascot of his high school football team and the honorary team number they'd given him for being equipment manager. He wore that jersey proudly for his high school yearbook. "Cougars 47: fight, team, fight."

Two minutes later and she had sent all his files, including his e-mail cache, to her mainframe. She'd sift through them later, or get Heather to do it. All that was left was a visual inspection of his cubicle.

Sparse pickings. Office supplies all in their own individual sections of the drawer, every paper clip in its place. Very few paper files. This was a paperless guy. Two interesting items. One, the latest annual report of Hawkins Computer Defense Systems. She held it closed and then let it open naturally. Just as she suspected, it opened to the page with Laura's picture on it.

The other clue was not so clear. A pink message slip in the wastebasket. She felt like a real detective, going through garbage. Right out of the movies. It read: "C at CSL 10:30." She pulled out her file on Edgar. Under Visa card charges she found three recent ones that said "Cafe San Lucas" and a long string of numbers ending with "5106609883, CA." She pulled out her cell and tried it.

Sure enough, it was the phone number. "Cafe San Lucas, can I help you?"

"Yes. How late are you open tonight?"

"Till two A.M., señorita. Would you like a reservation?"

"Um, I think I'll just drop by. Where are you located, again?"

"On University, between Shattuck and Milvia. Just a couple of doors down from the Nash Hotel."

"Thanks a bunch,"

"*De nada.*"

Maybe that meant 10:30 tonight. She knew that she couldn't make it, and besides, Edgar seeing her there might be stretching coincidence a little. But she knew someone who could be her eyes.

"Hey, Heather, aren't you hungry for some delicious Mexican food after taking that excruciating trig exam?"

"How'd you know? Getting psychic, like your boyfriend?"

"Warren's about as psychic as mud. I need you to do a little surveillance."

"Cool. Where and on who?"

"Cafe San Lucas, on Univer—"

"I know where it is; Berkeley, right?"

"Right. His name is Edgar Allen. He works at Hawkins. Think an ordinary-looking Matthew McConaughey type in glasses. He was wearing a blue Levi's work shirt and khaki trousers earlier today, and don't bother telling me that those don't go together."

"You're becoming an absolute fashion slut. I'll be there."

"Hurry, you have about a half an hour to get there. But don't speed. I just want to know if he shows up, and who, if anyone, he talks to. Thanks, sweetie."

"It's not proper protocol to call your special operatives 'sweetie.'"

"Sorry, Agent Four. It will never happen again."

"Hey, with a low number like that, do I have license to kill?"

"You have license to keep low, not be seen, and get the hell out of there if you start feeling creepy about anything. You got it?"

"Got it, not-Mom. So long."

"Over and out."

As Sally put down the phone she thought, *Not-Mom, I kind of like that.* She had done Edgar's office in nine minutes. She was running ahead of schedule. On to Laura's.

Sally got out of Laura's office just in time to get back to Greg's before the loop stopped playing. Laura's computer kept her completely locked out. Of course. She didn't really give it much of a try. Laura knew what she was doing.

No, the interesting thing was Laura's Treo 750. She must have forgotten to drop it in her purse when she left. It was password protected, but she'd let down her guard. An article about her in *SC Magazine* had mentioned her cat, Rocket J Squirrel. Too easy.

And there was her diary. Well, not really a diary, but she made some cryptic emotional notes at the end of every day. Laura was much more insecure than she seemed. "Wondering today if I can pull off this job?? I really make it up as I go along." "Fight today / G. He's thinking about expansion. It's all I can do to stay above water." "Wish we had more time together, with computer turned off!" "Do I still love him? Does he love me?" "We finally had a date. Yeah! It was wonderful!"

It wasn't the record of someone contemplating murdering her husband. On the date of the murder all it said was: "Greg out tonight. Going to bed early with Häagen-Dazs." Then there were no more notes. Grief will do that.

CHAPTER TWENTY-FIVE

G ot it, not-Mom. So long."

This was more like it. Hurtling through the night on the way to undercover surveillance of a suspect. Heather was already wearing scruffies, so she would fit right in with the late-night Berkeley enchilada crowd. She tore out of the house, knowing it would be a wild and hairy ride to get to Cafe San Lucas in time. This was living!

To the degree that it can be said that a Prius can haul ass, hers did. She got to the café in record time. The hole-in-the-wall Mexican joint had none of the New California, snapper-in-lime pretensions of ritzier restaurants like Picante. This was a lard-refried-beans, Spanish-rice, and damn-good-pork-grease kind of place. As usual, it was mobbed with fat-lovers, all relishing their high blood-cholesterol levels.

She bellied up to the bar and ordered a vegetarian burrito and a Dos Equis. She loved the cool new forged ID that Warren had made her. She had "forgotten" to mention to Sally that he had given her a new driver's license, along with the press ID: one with a few years added on to it.

Then she scoped the place, looking for men in mismatched business casual. There were plenty of them for her to choose from. But over in the corner, in front of the window, she spotted an excellent match, sitting alone, looking out the window. Long face with scruffy shadow, check. Levi's work shirt, check. Khakis, check. Glasses, check. And fortunately his table was on the route to the women's room.

As she cruised the potential Edgar Allen, she glanced down on the table where he was sitting. She spotted a folder sporting the Hawkins Computer Defense Systems logo. Bonanza!

On her way back to her beer she noticed her subject sit up and look out the window with real interest. OK, now she was going to spot the perp. She glanced up and freaked.

She spun around hoping against hope that the guy coming into the café hadn't seen her, even though through the window he looked like he was staring right at her. No, the streetlights were reflecting off the window. He couldn't really see in, right?

She headed toward the back of the restaurant. There were no exits except the kitchen. Big deal, she just became a waitress. She walked in and right past the two chefs at the grill. They spoke something to her in Spanish, which she ignored and kept going as far away from the front door as she could get, as fast as she could without running like hell.

She flew out the back door and past the Dumpsters. She was in a small back alley. All pretense was over, and she sprinted for her car. No one chased her, or fired any weapons at her. She jumped in and hummed out of there as fast as she could. She needed to put several freeways between her and Mr. David Cabot.

6

THE NUMBER SIX

FOR ESOTERIC philosophers, out of the conflict of Five comes the harmony of Six. Six expresses symmetry, balance, and beauty. It emerges when opposites finally unite into a third entity. It reminds us to see the inherent beauty and splendor that emanates from all of creation, once we let go of our prejudices and limiting beliefs.

CHAPTER TWENTY-SIX

The next day Warren felt fine, in fact, rather chipper. The reason Rose called him a high-functioning bipolar was because he knew he was crazy. This morning he was appreciating the cheery face of his bipolar disorder as he took his monthly three-thousand-dollar check to the bank to deposit.

Early in his adulthood he had received a large handful of excellent-quality diamonds. Many manics miraculously fall into temporary wealth. It doesn't take long for them to burn through it, sometimes only hours. Luckily for him, Warren had been in a down part of his cycle when he finally had the cash in hand. He had done two brilliant things. One, he bought Microsoft stock early on. Two, he set up an ironclad arrangement with Hal, his stockbroker/savior.

Warren paid him five thousand dollars a year to keep Warren's brokerage account number a secret. Hal sent Warren a monthly draw. But Hal wouldn't let Warren sell any of the principal stock. In fact, Warren couldn't get anywhere near his nest egg. He couldn't even get near the nest. Warren burglarized Hal's office, tapped his phone, and repeatedly and unsuccessfully tried to convince Sally to hack his files. So far Warren had lucked out: Nothing worked. So he got little droppings from the nest, but the egg stayed securely protected from his insanity.

Warren had started the day with a simple intention: bank, clean up his e-mail, and then begin the design of a tarot-centered blog so he would have an excuse to contact his old customers and remind them that he existed. But being bipolar is a little like having periodic attention deficit disorder. The interior of Warren's psyche was like that popular greeting card: "They say I have A.D.D., but they don't understand. Oh look! A chicken!"

After his banking expedition, he sat down for his third morning coffee, a latte at Cafe Mediterranean, or Caffeine Mesopotamian, as he was calling it these days, considering its new owners. He whipped out his cell, remembering that he wanted to call Vera and find out whether the depression that had hit him on the bridge last night was common. Just a quick call, a last sip of his drink, and he would get right on building that blog. Right.

Vera listened to his story and said, "Welcome to the land of the dominant. That was one big reason why I switched. We call it 'Top Drop.' There is something about being so in control that's hard on the old psyche. This odd sadness sweeps in sometimes, especially after a very powerful scene."

She'd been there. "You switched?"

"Yes, in my early years I used to be a dominatrix. It just got too hard, facing all those needy men. Then I met Thérèse, and everything changed for me."

"Cool. Well, thanks. I just needed to know if it was me."

"Warren, before you go, I have an interesting invitation for you. What are you doing today?"

This was the part where an ordinary person might say, "Sorry, but I have some very important marketing and promotion activities to take care of."

"Nothing much. What's up?"

"Come on over here, on your bike. We're going to a BDSM event unlike anything you can imagine."

"Sounds great. I'm on my way."

Warren thought to himself that this felt like déjà vu all over again. Here he was, back in the Marin countryside on his bike. But his passenger was a lot cuter this time. They were headed for the coast. He noticed a line of cars parked next to a pasture.

"Pull over here."

"Don't tell me this has anything to do with cows. If it does, I'm not playing."

Vera laughed. "Nope, humans only, I promise."

They climbed over a wooden stile and walked down a narrow path through the grass, heading for a clump of trees in the distance. The trees screened a little pond and an open meadow. A group of folks were standing around chatting, most of them very naked, or robed only in sheer scarves.

Vera took his arm. "Don't worry, it's clothing optional." She was getting to know Warren's anxieties pretty well.

She was in a short, translucent spring dress, with no underwear underneath, so she looked mostly bare. Warren regretted wearing leathers; he was going to get hot. But he didn't know these people well enough to strip.

Not entirely strangers. He recognized a few from last night's party. Including, unfortunately, his mentor Steele, wearing clothes, naturally. It looked momentarily surprised to see Warren. Then the mask dropped in place again and Steele nodded in Warren's direction. He nodded back, looking eminently cool for a guy who had absolutely no idea what was going on.

Vera said, "Interesting. Steele is not usually at these gatherings."

"We're just lucky, I guess."

This crowd had a very different feel from last night's. Someone was playing a dulcimer; a group of folks were making a circle out of stones, and a young lady wearing flowers in her hair and nothing else walked by, carrying a large plate and offering everyone some vegetarian sushi. Warren guessed wedding, but he was way off.

He noticed most of the crowd were talking to a large woman who was robed in a purple cape. Vera said, "Let's go pay our regards to Wendy, before everything starts."

"Can you at least give me a hint about what's going on here?"

"What fun is that?"

They walked over and Vera gave Wendy a big embrace.

Vera said, "I brought my good friend, Warren. I hope that's all right."

Wendy looked at him, a friendly face. Warren smiled back. She said, "Any friend of yours, Vera, is welcome. I'm so sorry to hear about Thérèse."

"Thérèse will be fine. Don't worry about it. Today is your day."

They drifted away, as others came up to greet Wendy. Her birthday? Warren was lost.

Since they seemed to have some time before the festivities began, Warren decided to fill Vera in a little about the progress of the case. "You know, Vera, we're all hitting dead ends. Heather can't find enough evidence to target a convincing bad guy among Hawkins's competitors, although she has a guy she would love to pin it on. Sally has nothing on Laura Hawkins. And while Steele is a weirdo, I can't make him-her out as a murderer. You didn't do it, did you?"

She looked at him oddly.

"Hey, that was just a joke."

Just then someone started playing the pipes. Yep, just like Pan. That was the signal. Folks started walking over to the circle of stones, only it wasn't a circle. More like an oval. Soon everyone was standing around the ring in silence.

Wendy entered the center of the circle and dramatically took off her robe. Underneath she was naked, except for a series of rings pierced into her skin in a line down both sides of her body. She lay down on the ground and the girl who had been passing out sushi began passing out strips of leather to each person standing around Wendy.

Warren looked at Vera, exercising supreme self-mastery to keep his face looking normal. He could see Steele watching him. Vera gave the slightest of nods, almost imperceptible.

Warren watched other people beginning to loop their thongs through rings on Wendy's body. Not wanting to look like the totally freaked-out guy that he was, he found a free ring and joined right in. Then they all stood there while a woman, who was evidently leading this torture session, started to speak.

"This ceremony has been done by native people for thousands of years. It is a sacred ritual, performed to connect us all with the divine presence. It was a part of Hindu tradition in the East. It was a part of some Native American cultures in this country. We are not gathered together to serve Wendy in her initiation ceremony. No, it is rather that she is here to serve us. Through her, we will all become one.

"Do not try to perform this ritual with your head. If your ego tries to figure out what to do, you might move too fast. Then you may rip out the ring you are attached to. Or you might move too slowly. Then you will not be carrying your weight, which can make many rings rip out.

"The only way you can avoid causing unskillful pain and unnecessary injury is to let go of control. Let go of being a person on the end of a line. Let that part of you who knows that we are all just one body take over. Do that for Wendy's sake. Now, when the time is right, the one that is in all of us will begin to lift her."

OK, now Warren was seriously freaked out. If it weren't for blowing his cover with Steele, he would have handed his cord over to someone else, someone more spiritual and connected with the all-encompassing whatever. He knew that he was the wrong guy for this job.

He looked around desperately, trying to figure out when was the right time to do the pulling thing. Exactly what she told them not to do. That's when he noticed that most of the people there had their eyes closed. *Eyes closed! Are they crazy?*

He looked at the sun glinting off the rings in Wendy's body. The rings started shimmering. As a symptom of his mental disorder sometimes he saw an acidlike hallucinatory sheen on the surface of things. It was an annoying by-product of his bipolar condition.

That's when he reminded himself that he was the real crazy person here. He thought, *That's right, I'm the whacko. Why am I trying to do this right? I might as well join in with the other whackos. What the hell.* He closed his eyes.

Something inside his mind gently pushed all those churning thoughts aside. Almost as if it didn't have time for all his neurotic conversations with himself. Something just came in and slowly, gently, began to pull on the rope. He knew that if he opened his eyes, he'd blow the magic or whatever it was. So he just leaned back and let this weird new thing inside him run the show.

He began to cry. He didn't know why. Like something that had been holding on so tightly ever since he was born could (just for a little while) relax. He could be a part of something so much bigger than little old Warren. And, in a funny way, it felt like it was he who was being held and lifted, not Wendy.

He had no idea how long the whole thing lasted. At one point he just knew it was time to let her down now. No, that's not quite accurate. Because it wasn't "Warren" who did anything. All the people there, Wendy, Vera, Warren, Steele, everyone, really became just one being, and the being knew when it was the perfect time to lift Wendy up, and to let Wendy down.

He felt the slack on his rope, and opened his eyes. Most of the people in the group were in tears. It really didn't matter what they were crying about. But it was good.

Everyone was basking in the post-coital glow of the ritual. Many were grouped around Wendy, touching and hugging her. Warren, a stranger, stayed on the periphery, and just soaked in the warm energy that enfolded the group.

But he was close enough to hear Steele say to Wendy, "I'll take you home when you're done here."

Warren headed for Vera, and cut her out of the pack. "Let's go."

She looked annoyed. "Warren, I know you have no social skills, but I still want to—"

"Steele is going to take Wendy home. That means no one will be in its apartment. I want to check it out. I've got to swing by my place to get some stuff. I can drop you off at your place. But we've got to go!"

"Oh, this sounds exciting. No way are you cutting me out of the fun. I've always wanted to see where it lives. Let's ride!"

They pulled up in front of the Academy of Correction, and again Warren locked down his bike. This would have to be a quickie. If Steele drove up and saw that rig, it would know who was inside.

Since last year, Warren had been taking lessons in breaking and entering from Max, a security specialist. Max was a close friend of Sally's, and was almost becoming one of Warren's few friends. Max owned and operated Valdez Security Systems. "Security" has many definitions, and Max's outfit could address most of them, from surveillance and protection to (it was rumored) vengeance. He used legal and illegal immigrants from Mexico and Central America: the invisible labor spine that held up California's agriculture, manufacturing, and service industries.

Maybe once a month Max would bring new locks over to Sally's for entertainment: Warren, Heather, and Sally all competed, under Max's tutelage, to see who could pick them the fastest. Each of them now owned a nifty collection of picks. Often Warren won.

After a Speed Racer trip to his apartment, Warren had his set of picks in his back pocket as he walked up to the front door of the warehouse. He was relieved to see that the dead bolt was just an older Schlage pin tumbler. If it had been a Medeco he would just have gotten back on his bike and driven off. He wasn't that good yet.

He felt inside with his pick. Only five cylinders, piece of cake.

He whispered his lock-picking mantra: "Delicate touch, gentle as a breeze." He put in his tension wrench and then, one by one, softly lifted each pin, twisting the cylinder with the wrench just enough to catch the edge of each pin on the ledge of the shear line: feeling for the click that let him know the pin had slid up just enough. In less than a minute the last one caught, and with a twist of the tension wrench the dead bolt was open. He used a thin, flat-edged knife, a little like a slender screwdriver, and a shim to gradually wedge open the door latch, and he was in.

Warren looked back at Vera. "Hope it doesn't believe in burglar alarms!"

"We'll find out soon!"

They entered the large, quiet main hall. Dust motes danced in the afternoon sun, and the bricks glowed with warmth.

"This is lovely. I've never been in here before. What a friendly dungeon. Very urban chic."

Warren headed for the stairs. "Not so friendly when Steele is standing in front of you."

The dead bolt on Steele's apartment at first looked a little more daunting, a newer Kwikset with seven pins. But Warren got lucky on the first try and racked five pins with one swipe. He got the other two in about the same amount of time it would have taken him to pull out a key and open the lock. The door latch, as usual, provided no challenge.

Steele's apartment was spartan. The furniture was made out of chrome tubing, glass, and mesh webbing. The hardwood floors were bare. The only spot of opulence was the kitchen. All-Clad pans hanging from the racks, stainless-steel countertops, Sub-Zero refrigerator/freezer, Wolf stove. This creature sure loved to cook!

Secrets are kept in bathrooms, bedrooms, and studies. There

were no home offices, and the bathroom was as bare boned as anything else. No drugs, no bloody ropes hanging in the shower, and, interestingly enough, no tampons. "It" was probably a he.

Before going into the last room, the bedroom, Warren warned Vera, "Look out; this guy is one obsessive perfectionist. If you touch anything, make damn sure you put it back exactly the way it was."

At first this room looked to be strike three. A single bed against the wall, a dresser, and a closet. Vera took the dresser and the bed and found nothing of interest, except that Steele wore tight bikini underwear.

The closet looked equally underwhelming. Shirts, pants, and a variety of leathers hung neatly on the racks. Boots and shoes on shoe racks on the floor, a metal box on a shelf. Aha!

The warded lock on the box made Warren laugh. Not much more complex than those on diaries. Inside was a ledger. Accounts for the school. Yep, there was his name in the latest class. Boy, this guy didn't make much money.

But on the back side of the ledger pages was a journal, written in tiny, precise printed handwriting. Here was Steele's life, week by week. Bonanza! Warren checked his watch. Figure that the party broke up soon after they left. Say Steele spent an hour at least afterward with Wendy. That meant it might be coming back within the next half an hour. Warren gave himself fifteen minutes, and started flipping pages.

"What's that?" Vera came over to him.

"Back off, Vera. I need to read this. Look, go to the window over there and keep watch. If you see Steele, then just yell to warn me. After that you might as well open it up and jump to your death.

That is going to be preferable to living through whatever punishment Steele comes up with."

On his bike, taking Vera home, Warren kept fending off her questions. Finally he said, "Look, Vera. I got an intimate and raw look at the inside of Steele's psyche. It isn't a very nice place. I am not going to gossip with you about it. He is very much a suspect, but I still have no idea whether or not he actually killed the guy, OK? Don't bother asking me another question about what was in the journal. It's really none of your business, and believe me, you would rather not know!"

He lay down early, but he couldn't sleep. The images from Steele's journal flew around his head, tormenting him like Pandora's evil imps. Steele had secretly stalked Thérèse for years, until the night she had discovered him outside her apartment building. She had tried to knife him. After the entry about that incident came image after image of him torturing and destroying her.

But it didn't end with Thérèse. Steele had twisted revenge fantasies about many of the people Vera had identified as the leaders of this loose-knit community of self-proclaimed perverts. Warren couldn't tell which of these stories were plans that were actually put into action and which were just products of a very angry, warped imagination. There was no mention of Steele actually killing Hawkins, but on one of the last pages of the journal the article about Thérèse's arrest was carefully glued onto the page. Under it Steele had written: "Vengeance is so delightful!"

Warren felt slimed, like he had come out of a foul sewer and was still covered in someone's else's hazardous waste. The shower when he came home hadn't touched the slippery filth that had insinuated itself in his mind.

Suddenly, he knew an antidote. He checked his watch. It was only ten. It wasn't too late. If he hurried he could make it to the Albany Sauna before it closed. A half hour with the door to the furnace open, pulling the rope to make steam, and he could parboil those memories away.

CHAPTER TWENTY-SEVEN

Damn, damn, damn, damn, damn!" Sally slammed her forearms down on the arms of her chair. Ripley looked up at her mistress, suddenly alert.

"I just can't get it."

The door to Greg's office opened and Laura poked her head in.

"Not a good time, I'm betting."

"Come in, come in. It won't make any difference. I can't even get to first base with this thing."

"I know the feeling. Look, none of us could. It may just be unbreakable."

"Look, the only program that you can't crack is one made by machines for machines. This ain't that. It's a software system all the way. It's got his fingerprints all over it. I've been reading his programs. He was good. No, he was very good. But he was no God. I will find a way in.

"I'm close. I can feel supervisor mode right on the other side of this ice. Once I get in there the whole system opens up like a flower. I can see how the rings are organized. I can see where the gates are. I just can't get in the first gate. Hell, once inside that I can just let my computer generate random numbers until we get it. It's clumsy and brutal, but eventually it will work. But I just can't get past authentication and authorization at that first gate. I wonder if it's four-factor authentication?"

Laura came around and placed her hand gently on Sally's shoulder. "Look, it's Friday afternoon. Most of the rest of the world is already heading home for the weekend. Maybe this is a good spot to take a break. So, on a completely different subject, what are your plans for this weekend. Any hot dates?"

"No, my boyfriend is going to school, and I am sure he's going to be tied up all weekend." Sally chuckled.

"What's the joke?"

"Just an interesting turn of phrase. No, I'll probably spend the weekend working on this. It's hard to leave when I am in this far. Of course it's hard to keep slamming my head against a wall, too."

Laura cocked her head. "Do you have to be in this office to work on it?"

Inside Sally, an interesting debate started. Venge was saying, *She's making a move on us.*

Psyche, clueless as usual, was protesting, *Oh, don't be ridiculous. She looks upset about something, that's all.*

Venge snorted, *Upset? In a pig's eye. She's working her mojo. And I kind of like it. She's a haughty.*

Sally told her voices to shut up and said to Laura, "No, I don't have to be stuck here. I could encrypt everything, route it through my mainframe, and then work off my laptop. As you know, my network is pretty hacker-proof. I don't think your security would be compromised if I did that. Why?"

Laura ran her fingers through her hair. Mojo or not, she looked sad. "Look, I know this is a bit sudden, and please feel free to say no if it feels like an imposition. It's just that . . . well, Greg and me . . . our anniversary was going to be this weekend. We had a room reserved at Sea Ranch Lodge and we were planning on having a perfect little celebration. Anyway, I still have the room, and I thought I might just go on up by myself. I wasn't really excited about that plan, but I didn't want to sit around in an empty penthouse all weekend either. Then I heard you swearing in here. I know this sounds stupid, but would you like to come with me? I could give Sea Ranch Lodge a call, to see if I could get another room for you."

Sally looked down. "I don't know if I can."

"Oh, don't worry about your chair. The whole place is wheelchair accessible."

Sally realized she was searching around for some kind of excuse to get out of going. Did she want to go? That was the problem. She really did want to go. But she shouldn't.

She was supposed to be completely devoted to getting Thérèse out of jail. That's what a real friend would do. And she was partnered up with Warren. He had finally decided to stop running and stick around for a relationship. What kind of double message was this going to give him?

Venge piped in, *Warren! Mr. Consistency! Every time things get a little too stressful for him, bang, he's out of here. Off on another little bike ride. And who knows if he'll come back from this one? He gets to be crazy.*

You are the perfect one all the time. You live in such a tiny box. Train your dog, babysit Justin, eat with Heather, go to work. Same old same old. Come on, girl, just for once before you die, do something completely spontaneous and unexpected.

For once, Psyche didn't argue with Venge. Instead she said, *You do need a break from this. The stress isn't doing your mind any good. It might clear your head to take a little "geographic cure" and go down to the sea. Just leave Heather a message telling her where you are. And don't bother calling Warren. This might be a good lesson for him about what it's like when he takes off without notice.*

Old Spider Woman didn't say anything. She just kept rocking in her chair.

Then Sally looked around at Greg's office. Everything was pricy: chrome, leather, and plasma. She had been through enough of his files to know that these two people had lived in a world Sally had never dreamed of: vacations renting their own island in the Marquesas or in an eight-thousand-square-foot villa on its own lagoon in Jamaica; this year, a new Maserati Quattroporte Gran-Sport; and that heavenly red wine.

She was proud that she was a renegade, a wolf snapping at the heels of the rich, powerful, and arrogant. But, just for a moment, she realized what she had missed: a life of quality, elegance, and sensual pleasure, instead of a life of righteous anger. And just for a moment, she wondered if she had made the right choice.

She decided to stall. "Do you have Greg's wallet?"

Laura looked at Sally strangely. "What? Um, yes, I suppose it's in that envelope the police gave me. Why?"

"Here's the deal. Give me a half an hour with his wallet. Bring his cell phone, too. If I get lucky with this idea, then I'll go with you."

"Good deal. I'll go get them out of the safe right now. Then I'll call the Lodge."

She left the office looking a lot happier than when she had come in. Sally noticed that happiness was infectious, now she had a case of it, too.

7

THE NUMBER SEVEN

THE FINAL results of the Great Plan of Creation are far from manifestation. We've got a long way to go. But we get little victories on the path to complete enlightenment. These small triumphs remind us that our struggles are not meaningless but just stepping-stones on the journey. Seven reminds us to celebrate winning the small battles and then get back into the fight.

CHAPTER TWENTY-EIGHT

Heather was back out on those mean streets, trolling for killers. Her first interview was with Tom Grabel, president of TS (Tomorrow's Security). It was in a blue warehouse in San Bruno. It had that *Blade Runner,* techno-grunge look to it. Sally was overdressed for this call.

She got out of her taxi. (She'd be damned if she was driving her car in this traffic nightmare if someone else was picking up the tab!) She never made it to the front door.

A door opened in a limo parked right in front of the building. She hardly noticed, but that rapidly changed when someone grabbed her arm. It was Hulk, from Cabot Security.

"Mr. Grable has canceled his appointment with you, and my boss would like a little chat."

She took a breath in to scream, "Rape!" when he said, "Don't even think about it. We know you aren't working for *Business West Coast Weekly* or any other rag. We know a hell of a lot about you. Now get in the car!"

He opened the door and gave her an expert shove. The guy could have bench-pressed her. She fell neatly into the waiting limo.

There was plenty of room for her to sprawl all over the leather seat and still have room for David Cabot. He watched her struggle to sit up with those eyes that had all the compassion of a corpse.

She looked at him and tried to put on an indignant reporter's face, rather than the terrified teenager's face that was threatening to show up.

"Just exactly what—"

"Shut up, Ms. Talbridge, or should I say Ms. Wellington?"

Damn, he knew all about her. Wellington was her stepfather's name. She'd legally changed it when she moved in with Sally. All she could think to do was be silent. It worked. Cabot started talking again.

"Yes, I know quite a lot about you. I know Mr. Layton is your trigonometry teacher. I know that the navy blue suit you are wearing is probably the one you bought four days ago at the Ann Taylor outlet store in San Leandro. I also know you don't need to go to outlet stores since you are independently wealthy. What I don't know is why the hell you are lying to me and my competitors about being a reporter."

It's always easier to adapt the truth than it is to adapt a lie.

"Thérèse de Farge is a friend of mine."

She paused. This had the desired effect, confusion. He didn't have a clue what she was talking about.

"So?"

"She's currently in jail for the murder of Greg Hawkins. Which she did not commit. I'm trying to help her get out."

"Oh, the dominatrix. Doesn't seem like your type." He still

looked at a loss, not understanding the relevance of the conversation to his initial question.

Heather went on with her lie, "She's an old friend of the family."

"So, you're going around looking for someone else to pin it on. Like me, for instance. And you come in with a faked-up ID to get me to slip up and accidentally tell you that I murdered my competition. Come up with a better lie or tell me the truth."

No way! "OK, it was a stupid idea. I'm sorry. I just didn't know what to do."

He reached over and grabbed her wrist. His hands were rough and calloused. " 'Stupid' doesn't even begin to cover it. I'm going to make this abundantly clear to you in a way even a high school student can understand."

With his other hand he tapped her wrist, her forearm, and her elbow. The edge of his hand was even more calloused. She thought, *Great! I have to be in the same car with Bruce Lee's fat white cousin.*

His voice was very calm, kind of like the doctor as he tells you that it's terminal. "If you or any of your teenage friends come anywhere near me or my company again, I am personally going to break your arm here, here, and here. In at least one of those breaks I guarantee that the bone will pierce the skin and will stick up for you to see. Is that abundantly clear?"

She was almost pissing in her thong. "Yes."

He reached across her and opened the door.

"Out."

She got out. Then he leaned over and said, "But honey, if you can pin it on Laura Hawkins, I'll buy you a new BMW."

Then he shut the door and the limo drove off.

CHAPTER TWENTY-NINE

I want those cards, you little twerp, and I want them now!"

Troy Baker was just as muscled as Warren had feared. He had that ex-con-just-out-of-the-joint-who-worked-out-pumping-steel-every-day-of-his-ten-year-sentence body.

Once again Warren regretted having his office on the corner of a city street. Anyone who could use the Web could find out where he set up his table. And then they could just show up and pound him to a pulp.

This was a crappy way to start the day. "Sure, buddy, sure," Warren whimpered. "You must mean those old cards I took from the fat guy's apartment. Look, I don't even want them. I tried fencing them, but nobody else wanted them either. Hey, you want them, they're yours. No hard feelings. I'll go get them, honest."

"Don't bullshit me." Troy had a voice like angry surf. "You tried that slip-away thing before."

"Hey, that's when I thought those useless pieces of cardboard might be worth something. They're junk. Hell, I can buy a nicer used deck for ten bucks. I was going to use them out here, to impress folks, but they're falling apart. Wouldn't last a month."

Warren watched Troy turn pale at the images of those cards getting mauled, rained on, and blown away, unprotected out there on that open-air table. Warren went on, "Look, it don't make any sense for me to run away from you this time. You know where I live, you know where I work. I run, and I'm toast. So just meet me, let's see . . . um, how about in that big parking lot beside the racetrack. I'll be there in my black Honda in an hour. That way you'll know I'm not up to any tricks. And how about five hundred dollars for the deck?"

That clenched it for Troy. Knowing Warren was just in it for the money allowed Troy to discount him, and therefore to trust him.

"Show up with the deck and I'll make it worth your while. I promise you."

"A-OK!" Warren complimented himself on his acting ability. God, he was good at obsequious. As Troy lumbered off, Warren dug into his pack for his cell phone. Showtime!

There is a large empty lot next to the Golden Gate Fields racetrack. Some of it houses horse trailers or trucks filled with bales of hay. It was a place next to the water where teenagers came to neck, parents came to teach their kids to drive, and developers came to dream about the high-rises they could build there. Most of the lot was empty today.

Warren's beater Honda was parked in the middle of the lot, as alone and vulnerable as a car can look. Warren sat alone on the hood with the sun beating down on his back. Right on time, Troy's brown Tercel came ripping up. Troy exuded his bulk out of one door, and a Troy clone, maybe even a little bulkier, came at Warren from the other door. Warren held his hands in the air. These punks meant business.

That was about the time Troy noticed a brown pickup, parked over by the bay. It turned on its lights and started toward the trio. Then from two other corners of the lot came trucks two and three. Brown truck number four came barreling in off the service road. Number five came out from behind a horse trailer. Number six must have just sprung from Zeus's forehead, because Warren didn't see where it came from. The pickups surrounded the two cars. Then all at the same time, truck doors opened.

Twelve Hispanic men as big as Troy or bigger stepped into a circle around them. Troy was the smart one. He stood still. His sidekick reached in (a little late) to pull something from his pocket. Suddenly twelve automatics were pointed at him. Looking at all that heat pointed at him, he stopped and slowly took his empty hand out of his pocket.

One of the men, a short, dark, tough-looking bald guy with a creased face and burning black eyes, said, "So, Troy; we understand you want a deck of cards."

Troy, still demonstrating his superior intellect, said nothing. But he jumped when a stranger used his name.

The stranger was Max, Sally's friend and right now the General of Warren's army. Max went on, "I have a problem, Troy. See, when a man is drawn and quartered, four horses are attached to a man's arms and legs, and then whipped until they each head in a different direction, ripping off a separate limb. Now the gentlemen you see surrounding you assure me that they could do it themselves. I don't think so. Maybe one arm or something, but not all four. I bet them that they were going to need the trucks. We brought the chains and the iron wrist and ankle cuffs. Inquiring minds want to know."

This time Troy spoke. "OK, we'll go away."

This was Max's show. Warren wrote the script, but Max was ad-libbing beautifully.

"Not good enough."

Then came the pièce de résistance. A cop car, lights flashing, came screeching up. Warren saw Troy's body sag with relief. Here were a couple of white guys surrounded by Chicano thugs. Just in time, Law and Order was showing up for the rescue.

A white guy got out of the car, and a smile lit Troy's face. He got ready to speak when the cop turned to Max and said, "I'd love to help you rip these two honkies into pieces. Which one are we doing first?"

One of Warren's very few male friends was a cop named Jim "Mac" McNally. With Warren's financial backing, Mac was in the process of getting off the Berkeley police force and opening his own bike shop. That process was moving slowly, so Mac still held down both jobs. He had cracked up when Warren called him to join in this charade.

Max said, "Listen carefully, Troy Baker, and you might just be able to keep your limbs. If you ever so much as whisper a threat to Phillip or Warren again, I will come to the city, knock on your door at 223 El Dorado Boulevard, number forty-four, or wherever you might have moved to. Then me and my boys will settle this drawing-and-quartering bet once and for all. Forget those cards ever existed. Do you understand?"

This Troy guy was an absolute genius. All he said was, "Yes." Not a trace of arrogance in his tone, absolutely neutral. Everyone there fully believed him. They could see that he had pissed a tiny spot on his pants.

Two guys backed one of the pickups out of the way and the Tercel tore out of the ring of trucks and then out of the parking lot.

After a lot of backslapping and laughter, everyone got in their respective vehicles and drove off. Warren headed to San Francisco to tell Phillip that his cards were safe.

"What are you learning about being out of control? It *is* the lesson of the Hanged Man, after all."

Phillip was propped up on pillows, looking like a resuscitated raja. He had greeted Warren's tale of the near separation of Troy and his limbs with a great guffaw.

"I don't think I'm learning much," Warren answered. "Having to be a dominant BDSM person is all about being in super-control."

Phillip was silent for a moment. He looked a little disappointed at Warren's answer. Then Phillip said, "It's ironic. Your life, I mean. On the one hand, these mood swings of yours can plunge you into an unwanted nightmare at any moment. There is a way that you are the most out-of-control person I know. And yet, on the other hand, you are completely attached to the belief that you are in charge of your life."

"Yeah, Sally said something like that. I imagine I am in control, but I'm not. Only she used algebra to prove it."

"Sally sounds like a very smart woman, much smarter than you will ever be, I'm afraid. Although she, too, has her failings, I suspect. You are under Sophia's influence right now also: the World card, Anima Mundi, the soul of the world. My guess is that you are still blind to the revolutionary influences that are about to rip away your illusions and reveal your true nature."

"Yeah, I guess." Warren hated it when Phillip got all significant. He decided to change the topic. "I have one question. When you were on your almost deathbed you kept saying something about 'the numbers.' What did you mean?"

Phillip let out a sigh about the size of Arkansas. "I'm not up to this conversation, Warren. I'll try to simplify. Numerology is a map that helps you understand where you are in the story of your life. Where you are in the little dramas and in the sweeping epics. If you know where you are, you can make better choices about what to do next.

"Forget it, I can see you're not getting this. Look, ask me again in a few months. Maybe then I can dumb it down enough for you."

"Thanks!"

"Look, you excel at action. That is your strength. Leave intuition and wisdom to those who have a capacity for it."

"Hey, I'm pretty intuitive."

Phillip rolled over and faced the wall at that comment. Then Warren's cell phone rang. Standing under the PLEASE TURN OFF CELL PHONES! sign, he answered it. It was Vera.

"Warren, your education is not quite complete. I think it is time you took a step into my world. I want you to come over to my apartment and get a taste of the joys of being a bottom."

"Ah, no; I don't think so."

"This is not for your enjoyment. Steele will break you in two minutes if you don't know what you're doing. Now, get your tail over here right now."

Warren thought to himself, *Hey, what could happen? I'm perfectly safe with Vera, right? Unless* she *killed Greg Hawkins. Only one way to find out.* It was another one of those "Oh look! A chicken!" moments.

"OK."

He hung up. Then, just in case, he left a message on Sally's machine telling her where he was going. Then he turned off his cell phone in case Sally wanted to disagree with his plan. He bid Phillip farewell and set off to learn his new profession from the bottom up.

CHAPTER THIRTY

The setting sun cast a pearly, buttery light into the long, glassed-in dining area. The wind off the Sonoma coast was kicking up whitecaps, breaking all the way out to the horizon. Closer to shore, waves relentlessly collided against the rocks and then took one final, joyous leap into the air before ending their journey across the Pacific.

"These oysters are delicious."

Sally was closer to happy than she had felt at any time since she had first heard Vera's scared voice on her phone. Absentmindedly she scratched Ripley's neck. This was a hard-won moment of peace. Even with Laura leading the way, the drive up here had been grueling, with nauseatingly sinuous roads, rock slides, and, at one point, a large black bull blocking the road.

Luckily, Laura had warned her to keep her van a little way behind Laura's car. In her navy blue Maserati sedan, Laura had led the way around curves, boulders, and livestock. Fresh off the road, they were decompressing from the drive with a glass of sauvignon blanc, a plate of oysters, and a sunset to watch. Ripley snoozed under the table.

"So tell me what all that business with Greg's wallet and cell phone was about?"

Sally clinked her glass against Laura's. "The cell phone was useless. But thanks to the wallet, I think I broke through the barrier that was keeping me out. I finally decided that Greg was using multifactor authorization. I noticed a credit card in his wallet for an account that didn't show up in his financial records.

"One of the portable phones in a drawer in his desk had credit card swipe capacity. I had the security video that showed him speaking into that phone as he swiped a card. I checked the phone records and found the only number he ever dialed with that portable was connected to an internal voice data line at Hawkins.

"So I dialed the number, played an enhanced audio of Greg's voice from the security video, and swiped the card. That dropped me to a new screen, asking for a typed password. I have my computer grinding away with random numbers to get past it. Then we'll discover the next authentication test. But at least I got past the front gate!"

"How long until you think you can get in?"

"I believe that by Monday you will have complete access to all Greg's files."

Laura turned and asked the passing waitress for another round of wine. Then she turned back.

"Sally, you amaze me. Thank you so much."

As Sally was taking another sip of her wine, Old Spider Woman finally spoke: *Drink all you want, girlie-girl. But you're sleeping alone tonight. I don't trust that woman.*

CHAPTER THIRTY-ONE

What is going on here?"

Tara stood in the doorway and surveyed the battle scene in front of her. Toys littered the floor. Milk was spilled across the table. Heather and seven-month-old Justin were sitting in the middle of the kitchen floor throwing mashed potatoes at each other.

"Did you know he could—yuk!"

Heather was hit in the face with a big, white clump as soon as she looked away from her adversary.

Tara said, "Wow, nice shot. He's not supposed to be able to do that for another year!"

Justin's cackles filled the small apartment. His next glob smacked against the wall.

"Lucky shot, I guess," Heather said as she wiped the gooey mess off her face. "What are you doing home so early? I would have cleaned the place up if I'd known you were coming back so soon."

"I got tired of my date. Figured I'd have more fun back here, and by the looks of things I was right."

The women started cleaning up the carnage while the man started chanting, "Wa wa. Wa wa."

Heather picked him up. "Justin, Warren was here a couple of days ago. He's not coming back for a week. It's Heather now; can you say 'Heather'?"

"Wa wa."

"You remind me of your grandfather; stubborn."

Tara laughed. "My brother was always obstinate and mulish. Now I can see that it's nature over nurture."

Heather put Justin in his crib, and turned to Tara. "I want to ask you a question, but it's sort of personal, so you can feel free to tell me that it's none of my business."

"Sounds interesting. Go ahead."

Heather hesitated. "Well, I notice that you don't date very much, and, ah, well . . . there never seems to be a romantic interest in your life. I was just, ah, wondering, is there someone, or are you—"

"Heather, I don't think I've ever seen you so nonplussed before. I'll tell you what you want to know. I find that I'm a bit of an oddity. I really am not all that engrossed in romance or sex or intimate one-on-one relationships. I've tried them. They just don't do much for me. I'm not frigid, just sort of uninterested. I like living by myself.

"I have great friends, both here and in Nwanetsi, my adopted African village. The one thing I was afraid of missing out on was motherhood. But now that I do so much of the raising of Justin, I have everything I could wish for. Does that answer your question?"

"Yeah, cool. Now let's see if I can get Mr. Toughie to show you what else we learned today. He can almost walk without holding on."

As she drove up to her house, Heather decided that she preferred playing peekaboo with seven-month-old Justin to tracking down murderers. The house was dark and Sally's van was missing, again. Bummer. She entered, disabled the alarm system, and walked over to the answering machine. Three calls.

Sally: "Hi, sweetie. It looks like I am going to be out of town for a day or two. I am going with Laura Hawkins up to a place called the Sea Ranch. It's on the northern Sonoma coast. I'll tell you all about it when I get back. I hope we are getting near to cracking this thing. I am almost inside Greg Hawkins's hidden files. Wish me luck!"

Warren: "Hi, girls! Oops, sorry, I'll try again. Hello, women! It's the PC PI here. Look, Sally, I am going over to Vera's for some extracurricular instruction. I'm a little nervous. This time I get to be tied up. I just wanted to let you know, in case something happens. I'm really not sure why I'm calling. Just wanted to check in, I guess. Well, bottoms up! I'll call later, if it doesn't go too late, and give you the update."

The last call sent goose bumps all over her arms. It was David Cabot. "Hello, Ms. Talbridge. If you really want to win that BMW, you might want to know this. Greg Hawkins was trying to sell the business and get out. He even approached me, but I couldn't come up with the figure he was looking at. His wife hated the idea and was fighting him tooth and claw. He told me he could manage her, but I kind of doubted it.

"Anyway, after our last little chat in the car I did some research on our dear Miss Laura Hawkins. Turns out she has a bit of a checkered past. She reported a physical attack by a boyfriend back when she was eighteen. The police did nothing about the report, as far as I can tell. Oddly enough, the same boyfriend was found strangled several weeks later. His killer was never found. Interesting, isn't it?"

Oh hell. And Sally was all alone with her. Heather called Sally's cell but got the "out of service area" message. Warren! She had to get Warren.

CHAPTER THIRTY-TWO

Up until now, you've been in control. My fear is that Steele is going to do an exercise in its school in which you will have to play the bottom, the one who is tied up and powerless. It would severely tarnish your image if you freaked out the first time someone put handcuffs on you. Agreed?"

"I don't like where this conversation is leading."

The afternoon sun was starting to turn that orange, golden hue. Vera had set up a wooden pole on a heavy metal stand in the middle of her living room. Warren was sure that it was much too lovely a time of the day to be messing around with this stuff. Especially with the way Vera was dressed, in a leather thong, a leather vest, spiderweb net stockings, and stiletto heels.

"You have to trust me. And you have to act like you are familiar with all these little toys, from both ends of the rope."

"Nice turn of phrase."

"Stop your stalling. So the safe sign is three knocks. I will be using a gag—"

"A gag!"

"Yes. And a blindfold and handcuffs, and maybe a soft leather flogger. No excessive pain, no scarring or blood, a little mind play. Is that clear?"

"What's *excessive* pain? And what about that negotiating part?"

"Look, Warren, I'm probably giving you a lot more information than Steele will. Stop dicking around. Are you ready?"

This was a side of Vera he had never seen before. Gone was the timid little waif. This gal meant business.

"Yes, ma'am!"

"From now on you will address me as Mistress Vera!"

"Yes, Mistress Vera."

"Stand next to the pole."

Warren stood with his back against the rough wood. She pulled his wrists behind him and he heard the click of the metal cuffs and felt the gentle pressure of cold steel against his wrists. Having been cuffed plenty of times in his youth (and once last year), he was appreciative of her care at not just slapping the cuffs on so tightly that they cut off circulation.

Then she said, "Close your eyes." He did so just in time, because the blindfold cut off all his vision.

"I am going to put a ball gag in your mouth. Both the ball and the strap that holds it in have been microwaved, so you don't have to worry about infection. Open your mouth."

He started to complain when she stuck the ball in his mouth. Then he felt the pressure of the strap to hold it in. Resistance was futile. He felt the rope binding him to the pole. She hadn't said anything about this. Then something was being tied around his neck. What?

The next thing he heard was her voice in his ear, whispering.

"You asked me if I did it. Good guess. I killed him. I didn't really give a damn about who it was. Just some john. Could have been any of the pathetic losers that Thérèse was servicing. It was always about Thérèse. Now she's exactly where I want her. And when they give her that lethal injection I will cheer in victory, for her death."

Two things occurred to Warren. One, this really wasn't a very well-thought-out plan for unmasking Vera as the killer. Two, he was about to faint out of sheer terror.

"What you feel around your neck is the perfect mate of the collar I used to cut off Greg Hawkins's air. He was so delighted that Thérèse's little slave girl was willing to do him for free. Arrogant jerk wad. It was a pleasure to take him out."

Warren felt a jerk around his neck as the collar tightened a notch. Not good.

"I will feel a little bad about taking you out though, Warren. You were kind of cute. You just got too close. I knew at the festival that you had finally worked it out. You would have to be silenced."

He'd been joking! He really had to do something about his warped sense of humor. It got him in the worst trouble. Of course, right now he was hoping he would have the time to make those corrections to his character.

There was another little jerk at his neck. He struggled against the rope that had him pinned to the post. Nothing doing. This gal knew a thing or two about knots.

He realized that he was going to die just because he was stupid enough to think that he could handle anything. What an arrogant idiot! He saw so clearly, too late, that he'd gone through his life lost in the fantasy that he was in charge of everything. Phillip was right, it was all about control. Warren had thought he had it and he really didn't have a clue. He had walked right into a lethal trap, not thinking twice about the danger he was putting himself in.

He thought, *Maybe I deserve to die. But I sure as hell don't want to! What can I do?* He felt another tightening pull. *Be calm. Let's take stock. My mouth has a ball stuffed in it. My hands are cuffed. My legs are pinned. I'm blindfolded. Not a lot of options here.*

He was so hungry to live. He really had something to live for. A lot of things to live for: his grandson, his lover, his sister, even his therapist. As he thought of each of them he saw their faces arise in his mind's eye. He started to cry.

In desperation, because he couldn't think of anything else to do, he knocked three times, the panic signal. Immediately, the collar loosened. He felt the blindfold removed, and he opened his eyes. In front of him was Vera's concerned face. Tears streamed down his face.

"Open your mouth and I'll take out the ball."

When she took out the ball, he kept crying.

He couldn't help himself. He wasn't going to die. He felt so weak as she unwrapped the ropes that he nearly fell over. She unlocked the cuffs and he turned and grabbed the pole for support, still crying.

"Here, sweetie, put your arms around me."

He clung to her and felt that wiry strength within her small frame. She held him up as he wept. Finally, she guided him over to her brown leather couch and he sank down into it. She sat next to him and held him as he sobbed into her shoulder. She gently stroked his hair and made reassuring noises.

"Yes, it's good to cry. Keep letting it out. Keep here with me. I have you, just relax."

That was where they were when Heather burst into the room.

CHAPTER THIRTY-THREE

No more for me, thanks." Sally pushed her chair away from the small, round table and stretched. "I need a shower. What are the plans for this evening?"

Laura stretched, too. "I know, that was some ride. Here's what I thought. We can go to our respective rooms and shower, clean up a little, and settle in. Then I'll give you a call in around an hour and we will come back to have dinner. Don't worry about the dress code here, everything is informal."

"Good. I keep some clothes in my van, but they don't include gowns."

Laura laughed. "You won't find a couturier within a hundred miles of this place. Sometimes they do weddings here and everyone is dressed to the nines. This weekend hardly anyone's here. I think that blue jeans will be just fine."

"OK, let's make it more like an hour and a half."

"No problem. And it looks like a full moon tonight. Maybe after dinner we can take the dirt road down to the ocean bluffs to enjoy it."

8

THE NUMBER EIGHT

YOU CAN flip the number upside down and it looks the same. Like spokes of the wheel of life, Eight represents upheaval, reversal of fortune, and change. It reminds one (sometimes painfully) that you cannot know the truth unless you are willing to face the opposite of what you believe to be true.

CHAPTER THIRTY-FOUR

Sally's in trouble."

Heather looked like the star of a high school production of *Medea:* hair flying in all directions and a horrified look on her face. Vera and Warren spoke at the same time. He said, "Heather, what are you doing here?" and Vera said, "What's wrong?"

Heather tried to answer both of them. She recapped the messages that had ruined her evening. When she told Warren about Sally going off with Laura it scared him—in many ways. What was going on here? While he had been stuck here, working hard, getting tied up and being scared to death by Vera's mind games and phony confessions, Sally was out there gallivanting with the merry widow. What were they doing together?

Finally he tuned back in to what Heather was trying to tell him: "No cell service there. I called Sea Ranch Lodge, but no Sally McLaughlin or Laura Hawkins was registered. That's when I tried you, and then called here." Vera and Warren both looked over at Vera's unplugged phone.

Heather started pacing. "Sally had your phone number in a book in her drawer. I'd seen her take it out to call you a week ago. It had your address. So I headed over here."

Warren still wasn't sure about all this. "OK, Heather, are you sure this is really the crisis you think it is? Cabot may be pulling your leg."

Heather stared straight at Warren. "And what if he's not? What if Sally is in real danger? Can you live with that?"

She had him with the glare. "All right; let's go!"

Highway 1 north of San Francisco was a hellish road to try to make any time on. The twists and turns had them all green. Road crews appeared out of nowhere, cleaning up rock slides. The moon was full enough for everyone in the car to appreciate the hundred-foot sheer drop to the ocean below. Guardrails were rare; deer, foxes, and owls were abundant and suicidal. Way out in the ocean, a fishing boat with a brilliant light gave them a point they'd be able to swim toward when their car went hurtling off the cliff. The Fun Ride from Hell went on forever.

Finally they saw the sign for the Lodge. Warren whipped around the corner, past the almost empty front parking lot, and into the rear lot. There was Sally's van! They pulled next to it and piled out of the car, all three of them running toward the front desk.

The pleasant lady sitting behind the counter said, "Oh yes, the nice lady in the wheelchair. They just finished dinner. I think I saw her and her friend going down toward the bluffs. Just go to the left as you leave the building and follow the walkway. When you get to the opening on your left, go down the stairs, and take the trail straight ahead of you. It goes right down to the point."

Warren fled out the door and ran toward the opening in the fence. As he spun around the corner he could see all the way down to the end of the point. There were two figures and a dog silhouetted in the moonlight as it reflected off the waves. The taller one moved behind the seated one. Then he could see only one person, standing motionless and alone.

CHAPTER THIRTY-FIVE

The moon's so beautiful tonight. This is a special place."

Sally leaned back in her chair and watched the waves rippling in the silver light. They were perched right on the edge of the continent, looking out at swell after swell, stretching to the horizon. The surf sounded like a gentle highway, quietly crashing against the jagged rocks below. The light from the full moon hid almost all the stars except the Big Dipper and one that flashed red and blue. *That's Warren's favorite star,* Sally thought, and felt a small twinge of guilt. She heard Laura move behind her.

The fierce shove was completely unexpected. In less than a second, she and her chair were airborne. Instantly, Old Spider Woman was in charge. She communicated in a language faster than words: *Grab the arms! Lean back! Keep the wheels under you! Let them take the shock.*

The shock was fierce as the chair smashed into a ledge on the way down. *Lean back, damn it! Pitch forward out of this chair and you're dead!*

The right wheel crumbled.

Lean left! Crush the other wheel!

A sharp edge ripped through the back of the chair. Then Sally's leg got caught between the chair and a rock. She felt the shock but no sensation. *Throw yourself back and to the right. We're just about to hit the water. Keep what's left of this chair under you. Straighten your elbows and hold on!*

She could hear her dog barking like crazy far above her. Then the shattering crunch as her chair disintegrated under her as she hit the rough, cold boulders and was thrown sideways into the crashing surf.

CHAPTER THIRTY-SIX

Warren ran harder than he ever had before in his life. There was no concern for his own safety. At first he heard Heather and Vera behind him, but soon he had outdistanced them out of sheer berserk fury and fear. He saw Ripley, Sally's dog, barking and then heading off to the left. He ignored Laura standing there, barely even saw her. His total focus was on Ripley. If anyone was going to find a path down to Sally, Ripley was the one. He ran full tilt boogie over the edge at the spot where he saw the dog's head disappear.

There was no path. His job was to get down this almost sheer cliff without breaking anything so that he could save Sally. Ripley had picked her way down to a tiny ledge. He jumped down to it, hoping the rocks would hold his weight. Ripley looked at him and gave him an encouraging *rwoof*. She had taken him as far as she could go. Now it was time for two-legged insanity.

He dropped down and grabbed the ledge with his hands. Then he swung his legs over the edge and began waving them around, feeling for a foothold. The first small rock he found broke out under his weight. The second one held, and he let go with one hand and began reaching for something lower to hold on to. A tiny beginning of a tree would have to do. Soon it was holding all his weight as he let go with his other hand and his feet were scrambling for a place to stand. Ah, there was the next foothold. Foothold by foothold he climbed and slid down the face of that cliff.

The roar of the waves was getting louder. He knew he must be getting close. He could hear Ripley cheering him on from above but no human sound from beneath him. He called out Sally's name, but all he heard was the unending grumble and swish of the breakers chewing on the rocks below.

Then the rock he was holding on to came right out of the side of the cliff and he fell. The shock of the water was intense. By sheer luck he had found a deep pool to land in. He went all the way underwater, scraping his leg, rib, elbow, and face on the way in. Nothing broke.

He fought his way to the surface as a wave broke over him, shoving him against the rocky edge. Then the undertow threatened to pull him back out. He reached out blindly and found a barnacle-encrusted rock to hold on to. He grabbed on with his other hand and pulled himself up. That wave had been the end of a set. For a moment, the water was still. Warren looked around.

It was a madhouse of swirling water. He pulled himself a little farther onto this small shelf that he was precariously perched on and kicked off his shoes. He was under no illusions. He was going to be back in the water soon enough, and he wanted all the mobility he could get. Cross-trainers weren't going to cut it down here.

He desperately stared into the whirling mess over where he

thought Sally should be. The first thing he saw was the ragged, twisted edge of a titanium wheelchair wheel. He could hear the suck of another big wave coming in, and this time he jumped up when it swept over the ledge, and let it sweep him toward the wreckage. He got a nice sideways lift and then almost got a concussion as it crushed him against the face of the cliff. There were no good choices down here.

When his leg got wedged between two rocks, he shoved it in even deeper. Just in time, because the drag of the surge tried like hell to pull him away from the rocks and into the surf. That's when he heard her.

"Goddamn it! Goddamn it! Goddamn mother—"

There was his little mermaid! He let the next wave hit him hard, and as soon as it ebbed he pulled his leg out of the crack and hoisted himself over three slick, slippery rocks. There she was, in the middle of that washing machine, holding on to a piece of metal she had jammed into a crack in the rock, her legs streaming uselessly behind her.

"Sally!"

"What the hell are you doing down here, you idiot! Look out!"

She was too late; the wave lifted him completely off the rock. He waved his hands around frantically, feeling for anything to grab, but the water was holding him up and away from the rocks. He knew in that moment that this wave was going to take him out to sea. That's when an iron hand grabbed his forearm and the fingers dug in. Sally held to her makeshift piton with one hand and Warren with the other and dared the wave to take him, all the time cursing like a longshoreman. She won, just by sheer determination.

Warren landed hard on her rock, and grabbed on tight. They had another brief lull.

He said, "Oh, I was just passing by, thought you might need a hand."

"She pushed me, that bitch!"

He just had time to say, "We saw. Let's get the hell out of here," before another wave crashed over on them. The water was freezing. They heard Ripley barking again, but this time the dog was over on the other side from where Warren had come down. He knew they weren't going to get up the cliff that he'd slid down. He hoped Sally's bitch had found them a better way out of here.

The water stopped pulling at them. Warren said, "Grab on to me and pray like crazy!" Two viselike arms wrapped themselves around his neck. He started to crawl with his human backpack. Mussel shells ripped his pants and cut into his skin. He bled on the algae-covered boulders as he crept over them. He didn't care. It was highly unlikely that he was going to die of blood loss.

Sally was his lookout. She would call out, "Wave!" and he would throw himself on the jagged surface of the nearest boulder and hold on to anything he could for dear life. So would she. Then she would say, "Go!" and reattach herself to his neck, and he would push himself on his knees and crawl forward, gaining another two or three feet before the next deluge.

Suddenly, there was Ripley, right down by the water's edge, barking like a homing beacon. Warren yelled, "Sally, hold on to me!" When the next wave broke over them he kicked off into the water instead of holding on. The wave had enough force to lift and shove both of them up and to the right at the rocky face just below Ripley. He grabbed for the ledge. Instead he got a leaf of kelp. His hand began to slide down the surface of the rock. But then the fingers of his left hand found a crack and he grabbed hard, fighting the pull of the water.

They were ashore. Sally let go and both of them pulled themselves out of the water onto the ledge. Ripley ran back and forth, licking both of them. They were both exhausted, hypothermic, beaten, bleeding, and bruised beyond belief. Unfortunately, neither one of them had time for such inconveniences.

Warren said, "Miles to go before I sleep and all that. Grab on, Sally. Somehow I have to haul you up this hill."

It was impossible to think that he could drag them both all the way up the narrow path that Ripley had found for them. Impossible, but still he knew that he had to do it. Heather and Vera were still in danger. With the help of even more generous doses of adrenaline and every other manic neurotransmitter he could summon, he did exactly that.

They got to the top of the path and found they were alone on the bluff. As he had feared, Laura had Heather and Vera. Now what? This was really starting to piss him off.

CHAPTER THIRTY-SEVEN

Warren, see that run-down-looking shed over there? It's a maintenance shed. There was a wheelbarrow leaning against the other side. I saw it when Laura and I came down here."

Warren took off, shivering. Sally lay there, shaking with cold and rage. Ripley stood over her, licking her cold skin. Soon she heard a creaking sound, and Warren lifted her up and set her on the cold metal. Well, it sure beat ocean waves.

"Go around to the right, there's a ramp. We've got to get to the parking lot. Ripley, *los.*"

Ripley fell into formation beside her mistress and they headed uphill toward the trees that encased the parking lot.

"That's her car, the fancy dark sedan." Sally could feel the exhaustion, just like those waves, threatening to pull her down into unconsciousness. She bit down on the inside of her mouth, drawing blood, hoping the pain would help her stay conscious just a little while longer. Three people were grouped around the car, illuminated in the silvery moonlight. Otherwise the lot was empty. Where were innocent bystanders when you needed them?

Warren called out in a cheerful voice, "Well, hello, everybody. How are we this pleasant evening?"

Laura whipped around. Now it was apparent that she was holding a small handgun on Heather and Vera.

"Damn it, Sally, what do I have to do to kill you?" she said.

Sally let her head loll over as though she were out cold. Ripley moved closer and licked her face. Sally made no motion to show that she felt anything.

Warren was a quick study. "Don't worry, Laura, she's all but dead. I found her body washed up on the rocks. Nice job. Now what are you going to do, stage a mass murder of all of us and blame it on terrorists?"

"Good idea."

Only Warren saw a tiny twitch of Sally's hand as she gave a thumbs-up sign. He started talking even louder. "Well, you might as well start with me first. What the hell do you think you are doing?"

Heather picked up right on cue and shouted right at Laura, "Let me go, or shoot me right now, damn it!" Vera chimed in by sobbing intensely.

Laura yelled, "Silence right now or I start by putting a bullet in the kid's head!"

In all that racket Laura never heard Sally whisper to Ripley, *"Zijdelings!"* Heather moved so that Laura had to shift a little to cover her, turning her back a bit on Sally and Ripley. Ripley slowly moved away from the wheelbarrow and begin to slink off to the side.

"Don't move a muscle, little girl."

Everyone froze. Then Warren moved a step away from the

wheelbarrow, and spoke. "Laura, let's figure a way to get you out of this without killing all of us."

"Shut up, mister." That approach wasn't going to work.

It was Vera, crumpling to the ground at Laura's feet, who came up with the best distraction.

"Why did you kill your husband?" she asked in a small, harmless voice.

"You should know that. You were her bitch, weren't you? Greg lost his balls to your mistress. All he could do, every day, was wander around in a daze waiting for the time when she would beat the crap out of him. He ignored work, he ignored me; hell, he could barely dress himself.

"Then when the SOB decided to sell my company so he would be able to spend every day serving his beloved dominatrix, I lost it. I'd had enough. I told him that Thérèse had taught me a few tricks, and to come over to his little private Loft of Delight and see what I could do to give him a thrill. I even used her equipment. Well, it was a short-lived thrill, that's for sure!

"I had everything handled, until you little musketeers showed up. The cops were going to find all the fake entries in my Treo. I would wipe all traces of Greg's plans to sell the company from the mainframe. Sally would be dead in an accident. Everything handled. Well, now the scenario is going to have to be a bit more complicated, but nothing I can't handle. "

That's when Sally sat up, yelled "*Stellen!*" and pointed her finger at Laura. Laura swung her gun toward Sally. Just then, Heather started running toward the Lodge. Laura swung her gun that direction. Warren dove toward Laura's gun hand. And Vera kicked Laura's shin. Laura didn't know who to shoot first.

That question became purely academic when a hundred and

ten pounds of growling, driving muscle, bone, and teeth hit her full force from the side. The gun went flying out of her hand and she was knocked to her knees. Ripley threw herself at Laura again and knocked her over on her back. Then the rottweiler stood on Laura's shoulders and bared her teeth and growled.

Sally said, "Please, Laura, just struggle a little bit. Then Ripley will gladly rip your throat open. I've always wanted to see her do that."

Laura lay absolutely still. That was when they heard a siren from a distance, coming toward them down Highway 1.

9
THE NUMBER NINE

THE TALE must eventually end. Nine symbolizes the end of a particular saga, endeavor, or activity. All the loose ends get wrapped up in Nine, and there is a sense of completion. But until Judgment Day, or the final extinction of the last star of our universe (whichever comes first), every ending also marks the beginning of the next story.

CHAPTER THIRTY-EIGHT

The radio was on, but he wasn't really listening to it. Warren was thinking about what the hell he was going to say to Sally once he got to the hospital. Then he actually heard the lyrics:

Driving in my car or listening to the latest news—
How the world is going to pieces.
Bombs are falling, hunger's calling, some say what's the use?
Everywhere I see angel faces.

Crooked cop—pulls his victim from a blazing fire.
Hooded boy—steals a loaf of bread to feed his mother.
Crazy man—is making sense on his vacant corner—
Crying the names of God to bring peace and order.

It's strange . . . how we love—in the middle of it all.
It's strange . . . how we give up—start all over again.

It's strange . . . how we're touched—when we least expect it.
All-ways we love.

He turned it off. It hurt. He didn't need some Joni Mitchell soundalike to tell him about how strange everything was. He felt panic closing his throat just as surely as Vera had done. There was a real possibility that he would never see Sally after this meeting.

When Warren walked in, Sally was sitting in her bed, looking at the parking lot outside the window of her ground-floor hospital room. She turned and smiled, a smile that used to mean the world to him. Her face was the color of a bowl of Cream of Rice, with very big raisin-colored bruises all over it. He felt like this definitely qualified as kicking a gal when she was down. But he was not very good at the long-suffering-silence bit.

"You weren't just investigating her, were you?"

She looked up at him. "Have I thanked you for saving my life?"

This wasn't going to be easy. He decided to confess first. "You know I came up here last year. I drove right past that yuppie haven last winter, in one of my flights from reality. I never told you about the day last year that I decided everyone in the Bay Area didn't need me. I was blissfully on my way to Alaska when I woke up. Rose called it Adult Runaway Syndrome with Dissociative Features. I know I'm not easy. Trying to date a crazy person can suck."

Sally turned her head toward the window. She looked like she was listening to someone else. He could see her lips move. Then she shook her head and faced him again.

"Look, Warren, you don't have a lock on mental illness. We all have twisted corners of our minds. I have a little advisory council inside me, and sometimes it gives me really bad advice."

"I can relate."

A long pause. The ball was in her court. The silence stretched out too long. He gave up.

Warren said, "So where do we stand?"

"Or sit, in my case."

"Stop sparring with me, Sally. What was happening between you and Laura Hawkins?"

"A little lobster, an unforgettable cabernet, and some oysters. That was about it before the shove."

Warren crossed his arms. "Look, Sally, last year I went out to dinner with an old flame and you iced me. Justifiably so. But I don't want to have a double standard, here. You had feelings for her, didn't you?"

"Oh, and you weren't attracted to Little Miss Vera, in her summer frocks and her leather boots?"

"Sure. She was a cutie. But I didn't date her."

Sally blushed. Then she began to tear up. He wasn't going to go over and hold her hand and tell her everything was all right. It wasn't all right. But he wanted to.

Sally finally said, "I blew it, Warren. I really blew it. I don't know what happened. She was all warm, and rich, and caring. It was irresistible. And you. You were kind of clingy and grumpy and busy with Vera. Don't you get it, Warren? I'm scared of relationships, too. Laura seemed like a holiday, a lark, a vacation far away from all the crazy stress of this murder case, and away from the tension of you and me.

"I know, I know—I got you into this investigation. And I *was* a bitch when you went out on that date last year. And I'm sure you were a perfect gentleman with Vera. But this time I was the bad one. I never kissed her, or anything. But I thought about it. And then you threw yourself over that cliff to save me. Oh, Warren, I'm so sorry!"

He couldn't hold back any longer. He sat on her bed and took her in his arms. She curled around him and wrapped her arms around his neck. They just clung to each other for a long period of time. Then Warren let go, and they faced each other.

He said, "Sally, I've learned something about control in this past week. We don't have very much. Most of what we do happens because of primitive critters slithering out of the mud, deep in our reptilian brain. They want what they want and they usually get it. Then we run around trying to explain to everyone else, and to ourselves, why we're being so irrational. It's OK to be a jerk, babe. I do it all the time. It's all about what we do afterward. So where do we go from here?"

"Where do you want to go?"

"I'd like to go back to July of last year, but so what. Look, we're both damaged goods. We're both scared of each other. And we both have a lot to learn. But I love you. I hope you still love me enough to stick with all the messes we can make together."

She threw her arms around him. Just then they heard a series of honks from the parking lot. Warren glanced up and started laughing. Sally wiped her eyes and looked out the window.

Heather was waving to them, from the seat of her new, white BMW Cabriolet convertible. Discreetly painted on the side door was the trademark insignia of Cabot Security.

10

THE NUMBER TEN

IT IS not enough just to live our story. We also have to make sense of it. Ten is the region where deep understanding intersects with direct experience. Suddenly the pattern emerges from the background and we begin to see our life as a progressive series of illuminations, rather than as a random collection of unrelated events.

CHAPTER THIRTY-NINE

Mac hit the side of his wineglass with a fork.

"Attention, everyone, I have a lovely announcement to make. Our favorite prisoner doing life for murder one, Ms. Laura Hawkins, just announced her engagement with one Edgar Allen. He will wait for her release to finalize joining of these two hearts in holy matrimony, which should be in seventeen to twenty, depending on the parole board. That should approach the Guinness record for the world's longest foreplay.

"Forget about them. We're here to celebrate our own announcement. A toast, to new beginnings right here!" Thérèse held up her glass. Her red nails glistened ruby in the sun. They matched the bloodred wine in her glass, a 2002 Napa Reserve Lewelling Vineyards cabernet sauvignon. Once Sally's taste buds woke up to fine wine, she had become an absolute snob about the topic.

Eight glasses rose of one accord to join Thérèse's. Warren looked around at his friends and family. What a long, hard road it had been.

There was Max, one arm around his beautiful, round wife, Isabel. There was Rose, already sipping her wine, instead of following suit with everyone else. There was Mac, in bike shorts and a tight, garish shirt advertising Pro Carbon Fiber Cranks.

Warren's sister, Tara, had one hand holding up her wineglass while the other arm was cradling his grandson, Justin. His daughter, Fran, was handing a very bedraggled toy giraffe to Justin and laughing. Sally was looking up at Warren with that smile of hers going supernova.

Warren, Sally, and Heather stood on one side of a picnic table covered with a damask linen cloth. The rest of the group was arrayed on the other side. Between them a tall coconut-covered three-layer cake gleamed in its thick coat of white frosting.

Thérèse went on, "We are gathered together to celebrate the birth of a new partnership. Warren Ritter, Sally McLaughlin, and Heather Talbridge have joined—"

"Hold it!" It was Sally. "Don't you dare forget Ripley!"

Thérèse laughed. "How could I? The namesake and founder! Warren, Sally, Heather, and Ripley, in inverse order of importance, have joined together to launch a new enterprise. Hopefully it will both make them some dough and make the world a better place to live in. Let us wish them unbelievably good fortune!"

Glasses clinked on one side of the table. As was proper drinking etiquette, the three who were being toasted smiled as the others guzzled the wine.

Warren said, "Now it's my turn. Last year life was easy. I had a weird little job, a friend or two, no, actually just one friend, right, Mac?"

Mac yelled out, "Yeah, but he was a great one!"

"True, he still is. I had no family, no ties, and a hot bike to ride off on if anything got too complicated. Then I met this preppy little chick and it all fell apart." He tousled Heather's spiky blue hair.

"In one month, I discovered my sister, my daughter, and my grandson, Justin."

With frightening precocity Justin called out, "Wa wa."

"Right, kid. Brilliant little bugger. Now, Yeats warns us, 'Turning and turning in the widening gyre / The falcon cannot hear the falconer; / Things fall apart; the center cannot hold.'

"But Rose says everything is just collapsing toward the center and, like the Phoenix, a creature is arising who proudly wears even more brilliant plumage.

"Well, I guess Rose wins. After we got Thérèse out of jail Sally sat me down and explained again why I can't go backward. Looking at my life in the past year, it's clear that a new kind of work is evolving for me, and for us.

"Oh, I'll still read tarot cards. I wouldn't give up that gig for the world. But the three of us, oops—sorry, Ripley, the four of us are going to start a little sideline home business. Find a niche and fill it, and all that. I don't think we'll do much advertising, just word of mouth.

"It should keep life interesting. And that's one thing I have learned in this past year. Love like hell and live full out! And so I toast our founder, Ripley!"

Everyone clinked and drank, except the dog, who just wagged.

Warren looked down on the decoration of the cake before him. There in dark brown piping was a perfect reproduction of their new business card.

Admissions, Advice, and Atonements

Don't go looking for Cafe San Lucas in Berkeley. It exists only in my greasy imagination. Likewise for Foster's Self-Storage in Oakland. And apologies to Picante Cocina Mexicana, which does exist and isn't ritzy at all, only excellent in a very California way.

The Sea Ranch Lodge also exists, and has fine accommodations and delicious dining on the coast for folks with or without wheelchairs. Come and see if you can find where our heroes took a swim! Maybe you'll even spot a shard from a titanium wheel.

Of course all the techie-sounding language and all the computer security companies are fictional (but I would love to see that jungle inside an office someday).

The wine, by the way, is no production of my imagination. The vintages in this book are probably some of the finest you will ever taste. Trust me on this. I have it from some of the best authorities.

In my other books I remind people not to use medications or make life choices like Warren. But this time I think he did a good thing with his money. Responsible monetary management, rigorous self-discipline, and bipolar disorders are rarely seen walking down the street together. Divorcing himself from his money, handing over his estate to someone else, and getting a stipend was a darn good idea in his case.

For any reader, please consult financial, medical, and therapeutic professionals when working with bipolar mental disorders, because "dis-order" hardly begins to describe the chaos they can induct.

My apologies to the BDSM community if any of you feel that I have portrayed you unfairly or made any mistakes with some of the data or language in your subculture. It is a unique world, and I hope I have done it justice. In that regard, the Power Room is roughly based on a real San Francisco public BDSM club, with a very similar name. Steele's Academy, the private dungeon in Marin, and the open-air ritual were all of my own fiendish design.

Followers of numerology may take umbrage at my liberal interpretation of the meaning of the numbers. They shouldn't—there is even less agreement about the symbology of numbers than there is agreement about the meaning of tarot cards. I adapted some of Dr. Paul Foster Case's material on numbers to my own literary purposes in exploring the meaning of each number. But I don't think I am that far off.

To my fellow tarot enthusiasts I hope I have brought a depth to your understanding of the cards the Hanged Man and the World. Phillip's deck and its origins in mystical thought are embellishments on existing history, and should be taken with a grain of saltpeter.

A final appreciation to all my careful readers: Every book has some unplanned inaccuracies, and it always delights me when you find ones that I missed. This book is like a Navaho rug, imperfect I am sure. The difference is that the mistakes in this volume are not intentional reminders of the balance of harmony and disharmony in the world but just "my bad."